Stranger in
Our Darkness

Stranger in
Our Darkness

a novel

by

Joyce Crawford

MOORE PUBLISHING COMPANY
Durham, North Carolina

for

Manly Wade Wellman
and his UNC group
and for my husband

There have been legends told in many forms, in many countries, about a Stranger who comes at Christmas time.

The Stranger of the stories never looks like the Christ Child at first. Usually he is old, and always he is sick and hungry and poor. He wanders through the cold, knocking at door after door, repeatedly turned away, until at last some good family takes him in. Then, inevitably, comes the Miracle. The Stranger grants some blessing to his rescuers, and then, before their startled eyes, he vanishes. And from that time forward, their lives are never again the same.

When you listen to the old legends you feel, perhaps, that no man asking help at Christmas time should be taken simply for what he appears to be.

Aaron Avery Sloane came at Christmas time.

Stranger in
Our Darkness

ONE

ELLIE COULD SEE AARON SLOANE FROM HER DESK IN THE DIRECTOR'S office. He was sitting in the central reading room of the Rockfield Public Library, just outside the office door. He waited quietly, bent forward on the straight-backed library chair. His thin shoulders were huddled protectively toward his chin. His knob-knuckled hands rested palms down, one on each knee. Some wrongness about him, there in the morning quiet of the library.

Ellie pulled the telephone to her, watching him.

He would be somewhere in his middle forties, probably. A narrow face, carved deep with lines; a high arched nose; cheekbones that jutted above shadowed hollows. Too-white skin. Hair a flat slate color, going gray, twisting, wiry, grown too low on his neck but combed back rigidly.

She shivered as she dialed.

He looked clean enough. The cheap gray suit he wore shouted how new it was. They must have given it to him when he was released from prison, she thought—the shiny hard fabric still held creases from folding. His shirt was neat, but too large; the collar stood away from his rope-tendoned neck.

3

His eyes made the wrongness about him, she decided. They stared ahead at nothing, pale blue and watery, unblinking. They held a look of defeat, defeat completely accepted. Defeat as much a part of the man as the shape of his bones.

There was a click from the receiver. "Checkercabyeh," a bored voice muttered.

"Send a cab to the public library, please," Ellie said clearly. "One passenger for fourteen eighty-one Walnut Drive." She put the receiver back, letting her hand stay on it.

Prison.

The word jumped in front of her eyes. It might have been printed above Aaron Sloane's bent head. Prison. Not jail. What do you go to prison for? Not just for being drunk. For what, then?

She sat staring out at him, chewing absently on the side of her thumb, wondering what he was. Her fear of him pinched her face. It was a fairly pretty face when it was not pulled tight with worry—a smooth, heart-shaped face set with widely spaced gray-green eyes. Even now, with the wide forehead puckered in an anxious frown, there was a childlike look about it, an unused look.

Ellie Clark was twenty-eight. Her name was Eleanor, but no one ever called her that. It wasn't a child's name, it wouldn't have fit.

Her fingers tightened on the receiver. Call John.

But John gets mad . . . Anyway Whit must know what he's doing.

But this is different, she thought, he needs to know about this, the children are there.

A chair creaked on the other side of the partition dividing her cubicle from the rest of the office. Whitfield Meade came around to her desk. Whit's small gray eyes were tucked in among a pattern of wrinkles. Creases marched up his forehead in horizontal ranks of concern, to fade at the balding dome. "You've sent for the cab, Ellie?" he asked.

She nodded.

"All right. Good." His voice was thin, high, like a woman's voice, or a young boy's.

He stood by Ellie's desk, pushing a pile of papers into a neat stack. "I knew Grace would want to do it," he said. "I knew before I phoned her. Grace is good with people in trouble. 'Of course he'll stay with us' she told me, right away, almost before I'd finished telling her about Sloane. She's always ready to help."

The little eyes warmed. "That's one of the reasons I married her, I suppose," he said. He gave the papers a final tap. "Well, I guess I'll go on down with him till the cab comes."

Ellie watched Whit's rounded figure bustle out of the office, watched him bend over the man in the reading room. She saw the two of them ease around the scattering of early morning old gentlemen at the long reading tables, pass the tall old library clock, start down the marble staircase. Whit's guiding hand was cupped under Aaron Sloane's sharp elbow.

Prison.

Grace Meade would always help people, of course, whenever there were people to help. That was why the Clark children were with her. That was why Grace had insisted on keeping them when Ellie started her morning secretarial job at the library. Grace kept them because she loved them and because she and Whit had never had children, and because she needed to care as much as Keith and Betsy needed to be cared for. And because she cared about Ellie and John, too. They had all been friends for a long time.

But this man, with his wrongness. From prison. Ellie stared at the telephone. This was certainly different. Anybody would call, it would be wrong not to call. She picked up the receiver and dialed before she could change her mind.

5

"Rockfield National Bank," the operator crooned.

"John Clark, please."

"One moment."

The so-polite voice. And the girl would be laughing at her, really. John said they laughed at her for calling so much. She was an office joke. Checking up on John, they said. Jealous of them, they thought. "It's your bloodhound," they would say to John, giggling. "What'd your bloodhound think was going on this time?" they'd ask. John was just a teller now, they could say those things.

But they didn't know. She wasn't jealous—not that way. She needed John. He held her up. He kept her safe. She did not know how to be safe without him. If you can stay on top, you're all right. But down underneath . . .

"Ellie?" John's voice was sharp.

"Oh." She gripped the receiver harder. "John, I know you don't want me to call, but I just had to . . ."

"All right. All right, Ellie, what is it?"

"John, there's this man here. He was here when I got to work, talking to Whit. And Whit's going to let him stay at their house. I mean, the man says he's an alcoholic and he has to get into some hospital for alcoholics only he can't till after Christmas and he needs a place to live till then, but I don't know anything about him."

"What are you talking about, El? I haven't got all morning."

She squeezed her eyes shut. He was getting mad. Prison. She hadn't told him about the prison.

"John, what's wrong is this man's been in prison. And Whit's sending him out to their house right now in a cab." She was talking too fast, and it was really important, but he wasn't understanding. She was just making him mad.

"Is he somebody Whit knows?"

"No." She tried to slow her words, to explain it to him.

6

"No, Whit doesn't know him at all. He got out of prison this morning and went to Milt Guffy—you know, the one who runs the AA here. Milt Guffy sent him on to Whit. Whit and Grace are going to have to take care of him, sort of, because he can't get into the alcoholic place if he's been drinking and he can't go that long without drinking unless he has help. It's some alcoholic center up at Cedarville. Connected with the mental hospital."

For a moment the line was silent. "Well, Milt Guffy knows what he's about," John said at last. "I'm not sure Grace and Whit know how much work they'll be getting into."

"But John I'm scared." Her words clutched out for him. "John, Grace has our children and this man's going to be over there in a few minutes and he's just out of prison and we don't know what he was in prison for. You don't go to prison for being an alcoholic, do you? John?"

"Well," he said after a pause, "being in prison doesn't have to mean the man's a maniac. I can't say I'm crazy about their taking him on, but I think I'd trust Milt Guffy's judgment. Guffy wouldn't ask Whit to help if there were any danger, to the kids or to anybody else. Just stop worrying."

She was gulping air now, trying not to cry. "I can't stop worrying, John. I'm so scared . . . I don't care what Milt Guffy says, I don't care what anybody says, I don't like that man. Oh John . . ."

"Stop." The word came to her like a slap. Then his voice lowered. "Don't start that, Ellie. You're not helping yourself or anyone else when you get that way. Now listen, I can't stay on the phone."

But she had to go on. She couldn't leave it alone. "I can't help it, John, why do you think he might have been in . . ."

"Good Lord, Ellie." His voice sounded stifled, impatient. "How would I know. Ask Whit. Let me do my job before you get me fired or something. It's all right. Trust somebody for once in your life, can't you?" The phone clattered as he broke the connection.

Slowly she replaced her receiver. She rested her forehead on the top of the typewriter and dug her fingertips into the smooth bun of hair at the back of her head. Why did she always have to make him mad, when she needed him so much?

But he was right, of course. Whit wouldn't do it if it weren't all right. And she'd be off work herself by noon. She raised her head and looked out to see the old clock in the reading room. Nine-fifty-seven.

The old clock was a safe thing. Dark, massive. Pendulum swinging its ponderous dull gold disc. The deliberate, tapered metal hands gave full value to the minute that was nine-fifty-seven. The minute mattered for itself. On the face of this clock it would never be dropped, never be discounted as—oh, almost ten o'clock. Noon would come in exactly two hours and three minutes.

She felt herself relax a little. She rolled a sheet of letterhead into the typewriter and punched out the date: "December 23." Her face eased into the tentative expression it kept when things were safe for the moment.

"Dear Sir . . ." One of the form letters. No need even to think much. Her fingers knew the words.

Outside, on the street, a horn honked. A car door slammed metallically.

Her job was one of the safe things. An ordered, mechanical job. Each paper in its obvious slot. Her fingers copying other people's words. Nothing she ever had to decide. No more ever required of her than she could safely give.

Whitfield Meade came back, rubbing his forehead with a plump hand. "Well, he got the cab," he said. He wandered to the window next to Ellie's desk and stood by it for a moment, staring out.

"What a life that fellow's had," he mused. "He says he'll

8

kill himself if he can't get help now. While we waited for the cab he was talking about jumping out in the street in front of a truck. Oh, I don't really believe he could do that. But you never know. He did sound desperate."

The defeated eyes flashed into Ellie's mind. "He looked pretty desperate," she said.

Whit pulled a white-bowled pipe from his pocket, turned it over in his hands, then stuffed it down in the pocket again. "Milt Guffy said that when Sloane first came to see him this morning he thought he was just another pro—a professional moocher, you know—with a darned good line. But the more Sloane talked the more Milt believed him, and Milt just doesn't get fooled by pros. He's known too many of them. He told me if he ever saw a man worth helping, Sloane is that man."

The pipe came out once more. Whit jiggled it absently in his palm. When he spoke his voice was higher than ever. "If Sloane is really desperate enough to want to get well . . . He'd have to be desperate, Ellie, to change. He's been an alcoholic for twenty years, at least, he told me. He'd have to be so desperate that even getting blind drunk doesn't help any more. And he wouldn't be able to change without a lot of help from somewhere."

The pipe stem tapped a nervous sequence on the window glass. "I think I know how Sloane must feel—how frightened he must be. That's why I do some things for the AA now and then—because I know." He turned back to look at Ellie. "I could have been like Sloane."

"Oh, Whit, not really."

"I could have been." He shook his head slowly. "Now I have a chance to help this man. If he can get through until Monday morning without a drink they'll take him at the Alcoholic Center. Just till Monday. It's so little for me to do, but it could make so much difference."

9

Ellie took a breath. "Whit," she said, "did you find out why he was in prison? I mean, instead of jail?"

"Well, Milt didn't tell me anything about that. And I didn't really like to ask Sloane. It would have seemed as if I didn't trust him. He must need to be trusted. But Milt vouched for him, and that's enough for me."

Whit paced back to Ellie's desk. "I don't know," he said. "The courts can be hard on alcoholics. Sloane told me he's spent most of his life in and out of jails."

He shoved the pipe away again, out of sight in his coat pocket. "Aaron Avery Sloane," he said. "It has a rhythm to it, doesn't it? I'm interested in names. Someone must have cared about Sloane once, when they named him that. Strange."

It was barely noon when Ellie raced the motor of the old green Plymouth and pulled it out of the library parking lot. She worked the car restlessly through the lunch-time traffic, tapped impatient fingers on the steering wheel while crowds of Christmas shoppers drifted across intersections. At last she broke free of the business district and drove fast, following the turning streets to the section where she and John lived.

She nosed the Plymouth into their driveway, tugged the brake on, and climbed out. With her coat flapping unbuttoned around her slight figure, she ran across the street to the Meade's wide white frame house. Without stopping to knock, she pushed through the kitchen door. Grace's fat gray cat ambled out of her way, mumbling grumpily.

"Ellie!" Grace called from her station at the oven. "You're early today. Just in time for cookies."

"Fine," Ellie said automatically. "Where are . . . oh, hi, Betsy-baby." She stopped to hug the little girl playing on the floor by the sink.

Betsy was fine. Of course. Three-year-old radiance glowed

through the squalor of mashed dough and cookie crumbs that coated her cheeks and her starfish hands.

Keith was fine too. From the living room Ellie could hear his shouts, grunted machine gun bursts, exaggerated groaning.

She didn't see Aaron Sloane.

"Chocolate chip cookies," Grace was saying. "And how about coffee? I'm ready for some, myself."

"Yes, please. Thanks, Grace." Ellie sat at the table, not comfortably, and watched Grace slide fat knobby cookies from the baking sheet to a plate.

Grace Meade was a tall woman, generously large. Her stomach and her ponderous bosom were corseted heroically beneath a flowered yellow housedress and a white apron stained from many bakings. Pink rouge and a dusting of flour brightened her wide cheekbones. Her hair, expertly waved and darkened, swirled high on her head. A few strands had escaped to paste themselves on her smooth forehead.

"You know about the man Whit sent out, don't you?" Grace asked. She kept her voice hushed, as if she were telling a secret. The voice irritated Ellie for some reason.

Suddenly the air in the room irritated her, too. It was warm and spicy, too thick, too soft. It clogged her nostrils with softness.

"Mr. Sloane—yes, I met him at the library," she said. "Where is he now?"

"Lying down. Worn out, poor man. He's just out of prison this morning." Grace arranged the cookies in a symmetrical mound. "I think he's afraid, Ellie. Afraid he won't make it through these days. It's going to be hard for him, you know." Her lips were pushed forward with sympathy. She took the plate to the table. "Here, Ellie, help yourself, won't you?" She picked up a cookie from the top of the mound and bit into it. "Oh, and Ellie," she mumbled around the cookie, "call him Aaron, why don't you? I thought it would make him feel more at home if we all called him Aaron." She turned back to the stove. "He needs friends so badly. Did you ever in your life see anybody so pitiful? If only we can help him. I think if you can't help somebody at Christmas time . . ." She let the sentence hang in the warm air as she took two coffee cups down from their hooks.

Ellie looked at the cookie in her hand. Soft. Soft; sugar and spice and everything nice. But little girls aren't made of that. Nobody is made of that. It's a lie.

Cover everything all up with sugar and spice, but what you've covered is still there hiding. Black. Not to be imagined. Nothing that ever really came to your protected life, but a darkness unnamed, waiting, felt. What you don't ever let yourself see in a nightmare because you wake yourself up screaming as soon as you know it's ready to show itself.

Only she hadn't waked herself up screaming since she'd married John. The nightmare thing had kept hidden since she'd married John.

Sugar and spice.

A man, a convict, asleep in Grace's guest room with lids drawn tight over hopeless eyes.

Stop it, Ellie.

She bit into the cookie deliberately. "Whit told me it would be until Monday morning," she said.

"That's right." Grace brought the cups of steaming coffee from the stove. "Whit suggested we might give him some odd jobs. To keep him busy, so he won't think too much about drinking. And to make him feel useful." She poured a generous dollop of cream into her cup and sat down with a soft sigh of comfort. "He's going to chop up some wood for the fireplace after he's rested. We bought a lot of firewood this year and then found out it was just a little too long—that fireplace isn't standard size. So he'll know he's really doing something we need to have done, you see."

12

She stood up quickly, and hurried to the stove. "I think I hear him coming in, Ellie," she whispered. She reached down another cup.

Aaron Sloane came into the kitchen slowly, his head lowered. He nodded toward Ellie, not quite meeting her eyes, and dropped into a chair. "Thank you, Miz Meade," he muttered when Grace set his coffee in front of him.

"Aaron, you've met Mrs. Clark—Ellie," Grace said. "Cream and sugar?"

Aaron shook his head and bent to the cup, inhaling steam from it. "No, thank you, Miz Meade. No, I like my coffee just the way it comes—black as sin." His smile only slightly lifted the corners of his mouth.

"I do too," Ellie said brightly. There had to be something she could talk to him about.

He ignored her. "When I'm not drinking I have to have coffee all the time," he said apologetically. "Keeps me going. Coffee and cigarettes."

Ellie looked down at the table. She felt herself blush. Somehow she hadn't thought he would talk about his drinking.

"Coffee and cigarettes," Aaron repeated. "Smoke all the time, just about, when I'm not drinking." He looked around the kitchen. "You wouldn't have any cigarettes here, would you, Miz Meade?"

"Well, I don't think so." Grace was flustered. "I don't smoke, you see—I never have—and Whit has his pipe . . ."

"I think I have a pack of Salems," Ellie said. She fumbled in her purse and found it. She held it out to him. His long fingers moved among the filter tips, touching, touching. Slid in among the cigarettes to pry one out. Bony fingers, bloodless. But clean . . .

"Keep the pack," Ellie offered. "I have more at home."

He didn't answer her. He lit the Salem and held it up in

front of him, squinting against the smoke, coughing softly.

"Whit can pick up a carton for you on his way home from work, Aaron," suggested Grace.

"Oh, don't put Mr. Meade to any trouble for me, Miz Meade," Aaron protested. "You're so good to let me stay here." He coughed again behind his hand, and moisture sprang into the pale blue eyes.

Grace's voice was soothing. "Now it won't be any trouble for him, Aaron," she assured him. "He'll be glad to do it. What brand do you want?"

Aaron's mouth lifted, shortening the crease down one gaunt cheek. "Well, if he wouldn't mind, Miz Meade. I smoke Chesterfields when I can."

"Fine," Grace said. "I'll phone him just before he's ready to leave, so he won't forget."

All at once Betsy wriggled up from the floor. Her sticky beaming face rose above the table's edge. "Cookie!" she squealed. "Keith! Cookies ready!"

The muffled gunbursts stopped abruptly in the next room. Keith came crashing into the kitchen. He scooped a handful of cookies from the plate and shoved a whole one into his mouth. "Hi, Mama," he mumbled thickly to Ellie. "When we goin' home?

"In a minute, honey. When I'm through with my coffee."

Ellie looked at her six-year-old with gratitude. Keith, with his dark hair that never would lie down. Keith, with his bare-gummed grin that all but split his face in half. Keith, not cautious, never tentative, for whom life held no half-measures. For whom there was either outer darkness, or total unquestioned delight.

She looked swiftly at Aaron Sloane sitting across from her, shaking the ash from his cigarette. A flicker of pity woke in her. Poor man. He really doesn't have anything.

14

Betsy pulled a lump of dough, gray and slimy, from the pocket of her red overalls. She squeezed it to a lopsided ball and put it in Aaron's hand. "Here, Aaron," she said. "I make cookie for you."

For the first time Aaron's lips lengthened to a full smile. He slipped the bony-fingered hands under Betsy's arms, his palms pressing each side of her small chest as he lifted her to his lap. Betsy snuggled against him. Her cheek rubbed dough on the front of his neat shirt. "I like you, Aaron," she said.

He patted the red corduroy that covered her plump bottom. "I like you, too, honey," he told her. His voice sounded full of phlegm.

Ellie's hands tightened around her cup. Her pity shriveled. She wanted to snatch her child away from him. Suddenly, irrationally, she didn't want him to breathe the same air her children breathed.

But he doesn't have anything at all.

She made herself smile at him and finished her coffee, gulping it down. As soon as the cup was empty she pushed back her chair. "Grace, I've got a lot to do," she said. "I'll get their coats." Gently, not snatching, she pulled Betsy away from Aaron Sloane. She motioned Keith to her.

"Those are fine kids you've got there, Miz Clark," said Aaron. "That little blonde-headed girl sure is cute." He laughed, wheezing a little. "She sure does take to me."

Buttoning the children's coats, Ellie bent her face to hide from him whatever it might show. "Goodbye, Aaron," she said.

Grace followed her to the door. "I think it's doing him a world of good just being in a real home," she whispered. "Don't you? And having children around." She sighed. "Those eyes. I can't get over the way he looks. The lines in

15

that face. Think of all the things that must have happened to him."

Ellie pulled the door open. "Let me know if there's anything I can do, Grace," she said. She took Keith and Betsy with her out into the clean December air.

TWO

JOHN CLARK LEANED AGAINST THE KITCHEN DOORFRAME BALANCING a plate of spaghetti in one hand. The telephone receiver was propped to his ear. His back was to Ellie as she stood over Betsy's dish, cutting her spaghetti into spoon sizes, but she could hear snatches of phrases.

"Yes, Whit . . . yes, of course you want to help . . ."

Ellie put down Betsy's spoon and buttered a roll for him. He took it from her absently.

"Well, I'm not sure what I could do . . ."

John was a lean man with his hair cut close to his head, the same dark hair that had come to Keith. Already, in his early thirties, there was a deep cleft between his thick eyebrows. His eyes were as dark as his hair. They looked serious now behind his dark-rimmed glasses.

". . . quite a responsibility . . ."

Betsy tipped over her glass of milk, and Keith, lurching forward to grab it, spilled his, too.

"Milk on my bread!" Betsy howled.

"Was your own fault, bubble-head," Keith proclaimed scornfully. "Mama, it's icky. I'm sitting in it."

"Not a bubble-head!" Betsy shrieked. "You a bubble-head!"

"Can't you keep them quiet, for God's sake?" John snapped. He moved around the door into the living room.

"Stop it, both of you," Ellie told them wearily. "Daddy's on the phone."

She took a towel from the sink counter and mopped the spreading ooze from table, chairs and floor. Keith watched with interest. "You missed some," he pointed out. "Right there."

Ellie thought how it would feel to throw the milk-dripping towel in his face. Instead she tossed it back on the sink and sat down again.

At last John came back. "That was Whit, telling me about this Aaron Sloane. No reason for you to worry about him, El. Poor guy—he just sounds sad." He twisted spaghetti around his fork. "I guess I'll go on over there. Whit thinks I might be a help. I'd like to do something for the man if there's anything I can do."

"But John, he's so . . ." Ellie looked at John's mouth, beginning to tighten, and didn't go on.

What could she have said, anyway? John, I don't like Aaron Sloane? I don't like him because he's hopeless, because he needs help, because he picked up my little girl? Because he's not like anybody I've ever known before? John, don't help him, because he isn't like anybody I've ever known before.

"I'm glad you're going to help," she said.

John picked up his coat from the chair he had dropped it over. He shrugged it on and started out the back door. "I'll probably be there for a while, El," he told her. "Come on over when you and the kids are finished, if you want to."

When the door had closed behind him, Ellie took her empty plate and his and put them in the sink. There was a pack of cigarettes on the window sill. She shook one out and lit it.

John cares about people. Good, her mind said, judging.

18

She didn't care, she didn't want to help, she wanted to keep out of it. Bad. Another badness.

Her badnesses were not the big ones, the dramatic ones, the somehow understandable ones. Hers were the cold small unloving badnesses that did not show, that she did not dare let show. That hid deep in blackness. That might be all she truly was.

I'm full," Keith announced.

Betsy was down from the table already, trailing two spaghetti worms in dripping circles over the linoleum.

Ellie stubbed her cigarette in a saucer and went to wipe off Keith's chin. Then she cleaned Betsy's face and pulled the strands of spaghetti from her. "We can leave them on the table, Betsy-o," she said. "They'll be here when we get back from Grace and Whit's."

She bundled the two of them into their coats, threw her own coat over her shoulders, and took them across the street to the Meade's house.

Grace met them at the front door. "Ellie!" she sang out. "I'm so glad you came along." She thumped Keith's shoulder and ruffled Betsy's blonde hair. "Run on in the living room, kids, *Space War* is on."

Grace was queenly tonight in a sleek dress of royal blue. The skin of her face, kept taut and unlined by the depth of flesh beneath it, glowed rosily through its careful layers of makeup. Life sparkled in her brown eyes under their well-arched brows. A heavy perfume hung around her.

"Come on in here with Aaron and me," she told Ellie. Her voice was rich, like the perfume, like the color in her cheeks. "Whit and John are back in the kitchen. They'll be with us after a while." She led the way into the living room.

It was a large, high-ceilinged room. From the stone fireplace flames sent their darting reflections over white walls and heavy, soft-stuffed oak furniture. Keith and Betsy ran to sprawl on the carpet in front of the television set. Aaron sat close to the fire, deep in Whit's favorite chair, staring at the blue-white flicking of the television screen. He didn't look up when Ellie came in.

"This is one of Aaron's favorite shows," Grace explained. "He watches it whenever he gets a chance."

Ellie sat on the couch stiffly, not tucking her feet under her the way she usually did. She glanced at the flat small figures on the screen, then at Aaron's face. The pale eyes showed no concern with the program. Aaron looked as if he were waiting. He brought a cigarette to his lips, his thin fingers bunched around it, and inhaled. The veins on the back of his hand bulged under the skin like fat blue worms. He coughed gently.

Ellie looked down at her own smooth small hands, folding little pleats in the hem of her skirt. She wondered if Aaron was uncomfortable, being the outsider here.

This was part of Ellie's world, her safe world. Even the droop of Aaron's narrow shoulders told of his not belonging.

She moved over on the couch and rubbed the arm of it with her hand. In the fireplace a log snapped, a new flame shot upward. Grace sat in the needlepoint rocking chair, watching Aaron, her lips curved in a calm smile. From time to time John's voice floated in from the kitchen, alternating with Whit's higher voice.

A safe world.

Safe enough? Ellie's hand tightened on the arm of the couch. No reason to feel unsafe.

The television figures faded, and music surged into the program's theme. Grace pulled up from the rocking chair. "I'll get coffee," she said.

Ellie followed her into the kitchen, lifting her feet over the old cat stretched immobile across the doorway. John and

20

Whit were sitting at the kitchen table. Pipe smoke clouded fragrant around them.

Whit looked up. "Hello, girls," he said. "We're mapping out Aaron's life for the next few days, I guess you might say. Milt Guffy told us he needs to be kept busy. Then too there is a small fee for the alcoholic center—not much, I'll have to find out just what it costs to go there. My idea was to give Aaron a few jobs and pay him enough to cover the fee and perhaps to give him cigarette money while he's there."

"That was what Whit told me, Ellie," Grace put in from the stove. "Whit told me we have to let Aaron earn what he needs. I said I'd be glad to give him the money and just let him live with us for nothing, but Whit thought the jobs would be important."

"Aaron is still a man," Whit said. "He must have pride. It would kill any pride he has left if he thought he was just a charity case. He'd feel like a parasite, I should think. I would, if I didn't pay my way." He slipped the stem of his pipe between his full lips.

"That's right," John agreed. "And by the way, Whit, I'd like to go in with you on the money."

Whit frowned. "Well," he said, "I don't want to drag you into this, you know."

"I want to help him," John said firmly.

Grace beamed. "That's good of you, John," she said.

John breathed out a fresh billow of smoke. "It means something to me if I can help him," he said. "Now let's see what we've got, Whit. There's the rest of your firewood . . ."

"And the woodwork in here." Whit peered around the kitchen. "It needs painting badly, and Aaron does that kind of work. He told us. I've got the paint—must have bought it—oh, five or six months ago, but I've never gotten around to the job." His heavy face twisted into a sheepish, little-boy grin. Grace smiled back indulgently. Then his chin firmed.

"If there's any time left after the kitchen job, John says he'd like to have the trim touched up on your house, Ellie," he said.

"I thought we'd let him sleep at our place while he's working there," said John. "Take some of the load off you two. We could put him in Keith's room and let the kids double up."

"Oh, that won't be necessary," Grace protested.

John was looking at Ellie, ready for her support. Her stomach tightened. All their eyes were watching her, it seemed, waiting for her to be one of them. "We'll be glad to have him," she said, because she must.

"Well, if you're sure," said Grace.

Whit blew smoke upward. "I know how that man feels when he wants a drink," he said. "It's like nothing in this world."

"You were never really an alcoholic, Whit," Ellie objected.

"Next thing to it, Ellie," Whit said softly. "Next thing to it. Close enough to know what it feels like. Oh, I was one of the lucky ones. I can enjoy a drink or two now and that's where it stops. But I know how Aaron feels, all right."

Grace moved around behind Whit's chair and smoothed his forehead with her hands, pulling his head back into her soft bosom. "Well, that's all in the past, thank the Lord," she murmured.

"I don't know where I'd be now if it hadn't been for those AA men," Whit went on. "Milt Guffy and the others. They took care of me then. They talked to me for hours sometimes when I thought I couldn't keep going without a drink. They showed me I wasn't alone. If I can help somebody else once in a while it's as if I can pay them back a little." There was a sing-song quality in the tinny voice, as if this was a speech Whit had made many times.

22

Grace bent and kissed the bald place on his head. "Come on, honey," she said. "Let's not leave poor Aaron alone all evening." She took up the tray of coffee cups and edged into the living room. The others followed in resolute procession.

Aaron looked up when they came in and twitched his slight smile. He took a cup from Grace's tray and settled back in the easy chair.

Ellie sat down on the couch again. "Well now," she heard herself say—a falsely cheery voice that surely could not be hers.

Grace's voice was itself, musical, carrying. "Betsy," she called out. "Keith. Come in the kitchen if you want ice cream. Fudge ripple—you both like that, don't you?"

John pulled a chair close to Aaron. He leaned back with an ankle resting on the other knee and his pipe held loosely in his hand. "How did you happen to come to Rockfield, Aaron?" he asked. "You're not from this part of the country to begin with, are you?"

"No," Aaron said quietly. "No, I was born in the South. Folks worked a little farm in North Carolina, but it wasn't good for much. I got out when I was fifteen. Never went back. Ran away."

"You ran away when you were only fifteen?" Grace asked, coming back into the room.

"That's right, Miz Meade." Aaron coughed and cleared his throat. "I traveled all over this country after that. Rode the freights. Worked on farms, mostly, at first. I'd go where the crops were." He looked slowly around at the watching faces, never quite meeting eyes. "I guess I've worked in every state in the Union except Hawaii and Alaska. Those farm workers were pretty steady-drinking people. I started drinking too—must have been what you'd call a real alcoholic by the time I was twenty."

Ellie shifted uneasily on the couch.

Aaron fumbled in his shirt pocket for a pack of cigarettes. Chesterfields. Whit leaned forward, a match ready in his hand. Aaron held the cigarette to it and breathed the smoke in deeply. He coughed again and the shirt collar pulled away from his thin neck.

"Later on I took to painting instead of farming," he said. "Made more money that way. You know, I'm a real good painter. I paint all day long when I'm at it, night sometimes, too. It's like I just get going and can't stop. I don't drink any, either, when I'm working. But all the time I'm working I'm thinking about nothing but that first drink I'm going to have. After a week or two on a job I've got a good big paycheck with a lot of overtime, and I take that check right out and blow it. It's like I can't help it. I can go just so long working and then I've got to drink."

He sipped at his coffee, taking his time with it, still looking around the circle. Grace started to open her mouth, but Aaron set the cup beside him and went on. "Those big paychecks are gone in a day or two," he said, quite casually, not quite carelessly. "Anymore I can't even remember what happens to all the money. I just wake up somewhere, and I don't know where I am or how I got there. Sometimes it turns out I'm in jail. Sometimes, when I wake up like that I think it would be better if I was dead. Maybe it would be better."

Ellie looked quickly at his face. It was as bland as his voice.

"I just can't take it any more," he said. "I've been this way so long—twenty years, I figure, at least—been in jails all over this country. I just can't stand jail. I'd sooner die than be in any more jails." He mashed his cigarette out and ran a hand over his chin.

"You people are good people," he said. "I wish I could show you how grateful I am for what you're doing."

"We're all in this world to help each other, Aaron," said

24

Whit. "If you can get out of this trouble—that's all we want."

Aaron cleared his throat and reached for another cigarette. "Guess I never did answer your question, Mr. Clark," he said to John. "Why I came to Rockfield. I move around a lot, you know, like I said. Well, I found out about this new farm machinery plant just went up outside of town there a way." His shoulder jerked in the direction. "I came on up and got a job painting there. Inside job, that one was. Thought if I could just work through the weekend I could get the whole job finished, and I talked the foreman into it. They locked me in the building and I painted all day and all night that whole weekend. Got it done, too, and it looked real good."

Grace's eyes were absorbed. Her bright lips held the sympathetic half-pucker. "What on earth did you eat?" she asked.

"Oh, I had some sandwiches with me, and plenty of instant coffee. But I don't eat much, usually, when I'm working. I like to keep going and get it done. Well, I collected my pay, and it was pretty good pay after that job."

Aaron sucked on his cigarette. "The last thing I remember real well, I had a bottle and I think I was trying to find a woman somewhere. Then it seems like I was fighting somebody, but I don't know much about that. I do remember a couple, three cops dragging me into a car and then I was in the prison here for a stretch. I suppose what the cops said about that fight must have been true, but I sure don't remember much."

Ellie looked quickly at her husband. John was quiet, intent, the line deep between his disordered dark eyebrows.

Aaron held his cup out. "Would you mind if I had some more of that coffee, Miz Meade?" he asked. Grace reached hurriedly for the coffee pot and filled his cup. "Well," Aaron said, "while I was doing that time some lady social worker told me about the alcoholic center and that I could go there and maybe get cured. She sent me to Mr. Guffy and Mr.

25

Guffy told me to see Mr. Meade. Mr. Meade was good enough to let me come here."

He dropped into silence, his head thrust down to his cup. None of them said anything.

A blazing log fell in two. Whit put on another from the pile by the hearth, pushing it fussily into place. The new log was damp. Smoke hissed around it, obscuring the flames.

John shifted his legs and stared at the pipe in his hands. Grace watched Aaron above the rim of her cup. Ellie chewed on the side of her thumb.

What could any one of them say to a man whose life was that?

A crash sounded from the kitchen, then a wail. Ellie jumped up and darted toward the noises, grateful to be freed. "It's the children," she explained. "They're just tired, I'm sure that's all. I'll get them home—you don't have to leave, John."

Roughly she wiped faces, buttoned coats and led the children, still complaining, out the kitchen door and across the street to home.

Much later, past midnight, she lay in bed, alone, staring up at the ceiling light, waiting. The light bulb glowed through a square of plastic with a thin tracery of white leaves around its edge. A heap of dead insects shadowed the center of the square. She watched one small, doomed black bug zig-zag in and out of the shadow. She hated overhead lights. Harsh lights, unkind . . . But she could not make the effort to turn it off.

Poor Aaron, she thought. She formed the words carefully in her mind, as if she were saying them aloud. Poor Aaron. He needs us, all of us, to hold him up.

She closed her eyes and let some of her tightness go.

The back door clicked open and shut, and John came

quietly into the bedroom. He dropped his coat over a chair and sank down on the edge of the bed. The line between his eyes was a straight shadow. "What a mess of a life that poor guy's got," he said. He pulled off his tie and threw it in the direction of the bureau.

"Maybe being here will make things different for him," said Ellie.

"I don't know," John answered. "I hope so. God, I hope so."

Ellie reached out and touched his shoulder. John. So good. So caring. Warmth gathered in her. She moved closer and put her arm around him.

He didn't turn. "You know, he talked a lot more about himself after you left," he said. "He was married once. When he was in his thirties he got married to a girl who was just seventeen. He talked about her a lot this evening. They had a couple of children, both girls. But finally his wife divorced him."

"Oh," Ellie said. She leaned her head on John's shoulder. The warmness spread through her body and she welcomed it, feeling a distant pity for Aaron and all who were alone. She rubbed her head under her husband's chin, mussing her loosened hair.

"He hasn't seen those little girls for years," John went on. His wife won't let him visit them at all. When he was telling us about them he couldn't even remember how old they are."

He stood up, not aware of her arms. She lay back and watched his spare body move and bend as he undressed. She could almost feel it now, firm against her skin.

Forget Aaron Sloane, she tried to tell him, with her eyes, with her ready presence, not able to say it in words. Just for a while, forget him. I'm here.

He turned out the light and got into bed. She nestled to him, ran her hand down his tense arm. He lay unmoving in the dark. "I've never been able to help anybody," he said, more to himself than to her. "I've never mattered to anyone's life. I've never done anything that mattered. When Don got shot down over Korea, and I was just a kid and Don was the greatest brother a kid could have—I used to think that was the biggest thing a person could do—use his life so it meant something, even if he got killed."

He sat up, staring out the window. "I've never done anything that meant anything. Nothing I've done has ever made a damn bit of difference. To anybody."

"You make a difference to me," she told him urgently. "John—oh—can't I tell you how much you matter to me? I'd fall apart if it weren't for you. Don't you know that?"

It was as if he didn't hear her. "I can help this man Aaron, I think," he declared. "Maybe if I can help him now . . . if we all can help him . . . that would be something . . ."

Ellie turned on her side, away from him. The warmth within her changed, roughened, shaped itself into a helpless anger. Why Aaron Sloane? Do you have to be a down-and-out umpteen-time loser?

Her hands clutched to fists under the covers. Stop that, Ellie Clark, she told herself. Aaron needs everything there is to need. John cares that he does. So care, Ellie Clark, care too. She shut her eyes.

John talked on, musingly, about his brother, about Aaron. About what life could be, perhaps, but never really is.

Little by little as she lay still his voice thinned out to a thread and melted into her dream.

THREE

GRACE DUG POWERFULLY INTO THE MOUND OF DOUGH BEFORE HER, pulled it half over on itself, slapped it to a new position and dug again. The dough plumped up around her hands and filled the room with its yeasty smell. From the table Ellie watched dully.

"How long do you suppose it's been since Aaron had a real Christmas dinner?" Grace wondered aloud. "He told me he was in jail some place last Christmas."

"I guess this will be one meal he'll remember," Ellie said. She knew her voice was blank. She felt blank. Wrung-out.

The day before Christmas. She ought to be home, cooking, cleaning, getting ready. Doing all the things you were supposed to do before Christmas. But Grace's kitchen was warm. Here was the calm, orderly feeling of work going on, life going on.

There was no such feeling in her own house, not even when she was busy in it. At home, too much depended on her.

The gray cat wandered over to her, gathered itself in, and with a single effortless leap, was on her knees. Absently she stroked its fur. Its eyelids floated shut and it lay purring comfortably under her hand.

Grace plopped the dough into a bowl, covered it with a damp towel and pushed it to the back of the counter. The bowl was heavy earthenware, the color of creamed coffee, the color the yeast smell would be if smells had color.

Today Grace wore a crisp print housedress under the enveloping apron. Her face was pink with heat and pleasure, her brown eyes were alive. Suddenly there was a beauty in Grace. Ellie had never noticed it before.

Grace meant capability and comfort. Her very bigness was comforting. Now, bending over the counter, riffling through the recipe cards in a battered tin file box, Grace was beautiful. Big-bosomed, energetic, blooming. Generous, filled with life, with love enough and more than enough to reach out to a desperate man.

Ellie looked down at her own slight bust, pushing out so timidly the blue sweater she wore. At the hips she had always kept so trim. Would she have more to give if she could be like Grace?

"Well, that takes care of the rolls," Grace was saying. "I'd better get those pies out of the way. Oh, and more cookies." She stooped and pulled another coffee-colored bowl from the cabinet beneath the sink. "You know, Aaron really liked those chocolate chip cookies I made him yesterday. They're gone already. I want to have something sweet around for him to nibble on whenever he feels like it. I think sweet things can help sometimes, don't you?"

She cracked an egg on the edge of the bowl and dropped it in neatly from the split halves of its shell. "Ellie," she said earnestly, "when I see Aaron, with that look of his—you know—I wish I could take care of him so well it would make up for everything that's ever happened to him."

The back door swung open and Aaron shuffled in, his arms piled high with logs. A blast of icy air followed him, slicing through the oven-warmth of the kitchen. He wore Whit's heavy plaid wool shirt and work pants. The pants were too big and he had belted them in a neat fold at the waist. "Good morning, Miz Clark," he said in his unemphatic voice. "Miz Meade, could I have some more coffee? It sure would go good after I get this fire started."

"Why of course, Aaron," said Grace. "Right away." She hurried to the stove. "You'll have some more, won't you, Ellie?"

"Please." Ellie reached for her cup. When she moved her hand the old cat looked up in reproach. It dropped from her lap and twisted soundlessly out of the kitchen.

Aaron carried the logs to the next room. There were sounds of crackling paper and twigs snapping, and the savory sharp smell of smoke drifted in. Betsy's head, lost under a huge flowered hat of Grace's, poked in through the doorway. "Aaron make fire!" she announced importantly. "Keith help. I go help too now. 'Bye." The gaudy flowers wobbled out of sight.

Grace brought the coffee pot to the table. "Aaron loves those children, Ellie," she said. She smiled gently. "They're good for him, too. I just know they are."

She lowered her voice. "Ellie, do you know what he's doing? He's been making Christmas presents for them. He's been carving little boats out of some of the firewood. They're just perfect—every detail. The kids'll be wild about them. He's an artist."

"That's nice," Ellie said, and wondered why it was hard to say.

She looked at the doorway uneasily. Then, not knowing really why she had to do it, she got up and went the way Betsy had gone, out into the living room.

The fire was well started. Tall flames poured upward to the brightened chimney. Little newborn flames fluttered around the ends of the logs. Keith, quiet for once, lay on his stomach before the fire. Aaron Sloane was not there. And Betsy was gone.

Ellie's uneasiness sharpened, edged toward fear. "Keith," she said quickly, "where did Betsy go?"

He didn't look around. "Outside," he said. "Aaron took her out. Said he wanted to show her something."

"Why didn't you go, too?"

"Ahhh, I don't know. He just asked Betsy."

Keith lifted an invisible rifle and aimed it at a log. "Kapow!" he shouted suddenly.

Ellie ran to the front door and tugged it open, fear twisting in her now. Prison . . . Show her something . . .

There was only the bare porch outside, the empty front yard, the vacant street. She slammed the door behind her and ran down the steps and around the house.

Panic . . . Pictures, headlines, throbbing in a whirlwind in her brain. Betsy, Aaron . . .

There, beside the garage, Grace's big flowered hat, abandoned on dead grass . . .

Oh God no . . .

She ran, so slowly it seemed—as in a dream, with failure predetermined—yet ran as fast as she could.

Inside the garage it was dark. Helplessly she stopped and blinked and let her eyes adjust.

They were there. Far in a corner, beyond the pile of logs. Betsy squatted on the concrete floor, her coat unbuttoned. Aaron bent above her, reaching . . .

"Betsy!" Ellie heard her own voice burst the soft dusk.

Betsy looked up. "Mama!" she exclaimed happily. "Aaron give me wood! Lots and lots! I make things with it!"

Ellie came closer. There on the floor was a heap of chips from the logs Aaron had been cutting. White chips, sweet smelling.

Aaron straightened and smiled his piece of a smile. "I

32

thought your little girl might like these chips, Miz Clark," he said. "Most kids her size get a kick out of something like that to play with. We're just bringing them in."

"Oh," Ellie said. Her heart was still racing. The panic died down slowly, congealed to a hot, embarrassed sickness inside her. "I didn't know. I just wondered . . . where Betsy was." She made herself smile. "Thank you, Aaron," she said.

Shivering in the cold she hadn't felt till now, she left the garage and went back in to Grace's kitchen.

Before long Aaron came, dusting his hands down the sides of the old pants. "Your little girl took her wood chips in the other room there, Miz Clark," he said. He sat down and drained his coffee cup with a quick short motion. "That coffee goes good."

He handed the cup to Grace. Beaming, she filled it.

Still embarrassed, Ellie sipped at her own coffee. She watched Aaron's white fingers fumble with a new pack of Chesterfields. His eyelids wrinkled, the colorless lashes quivered. Finally he worked out a cigarette, jammed it into his mouth, and patted the pockets of the oversized pants for a match. Ellie held her lighter forward. The cigarette trembled as he held it to the flame. He inhaled deeply. Smoke threaded upward from his lips and his narrow nostrils. "Thanks, Miz Clark," he said. "Have to smoke all the time, just about, when I'm not drinking."

For a moment he smoked in silence. Then he jerked his chair back and paced around the kitchen, studying the baseboards. He shook the cigarette at a bare patch.

"Mr. Meade sure was right about this woodwork needing painting, Miz Meade," he said. "Must have not been done for a long time."

Grace's cheeks grew pinker, then faded. "Whit's been going to get to it," she explained. "But if you could paint it, Aaron, it would save him a lot of trouble."

"Would you mind if I see what kind of paint Mr. Meade has?" Aaron asked. "I can't use just anything if I'm going to do a good job for you."

Grace pointed toward the basement. "I think it's all down there," she said. "Whit had bought something for the kitchen —but of course you can use whatever we have. We were going to make it ivory again, you know."

Aaron nodded. He clumped down the basement stairs, smoke streaming behind him.

"He isn't going to work in here now, while you're cooking, is he?" Ellie asked.

"Oh dear," Grace said. "I really hadn't thought about that." She looked at the half-stirred cookie dough in its bowl on the counter. "It will be a mess, won't it?" She glanced toward the basement door. "Well, it doesn't matter. Poor man. He does have to keep busy, Ellie—Whit was right. Did you see? He couldn't sit still for five minutes just now."

She got up and brushed a strand of dark hair from her forehead with the back of her plump arm, dusting a flour streak onto her face. "Maybe I can get these cookies in the oven at least, while he finds the paint and brushes and things," she said. She set the bowl under the electric mixer.

Aaron's voice rose up above the mixer's whirr. "Oh, Miz Meade."

Ellie jumped. She hadn't heard him come back.

"You haven't got any paint down there that's much good," he said. "I sure am glad you let me look at it. No wonder those baseboards need doing over if that's what you used before."

Grace turned the mixer off. Her forehead crinkled. "I think it is the same kind of paint that was on here," she said.

Aaron squatted and ran a finger along a strip of baseboard. One side of his mouth raised slightly around the drooping cigarette. "Well, whoever it was sold it to Mr. Meade sure

34

cheated him," he said. "Now here's the way it is, Miz Meade—a paint job can't be any better than the paint you use. If you want a good job done you can't put on just anything. This stuff wears right off."

He scraped at the board with a yellowed fingernail and a skin of ivory enamel curled up.

"Oh dear," Grace said. "I see what you mean. You must know a lot about paint, Aaron."

"Well, as a matter of fact I do." He straightened and brought a fresh cigarette from his pocket.

Ellie's lighter was ready. He bent over it and nodded thanks. "Now, Miz Meade," he said, "I can go ahead with what paint you have if you want me to. Or if you'd rather, I can see if Mr. Meade would want to go downtown and get some that'll last you a while. It's whatever you say." He stood waiting, blowing the smoke away from his face.

Grace looked at him thoughtfully. "I think we ought to take your advice about the paint, Aaron," she said. "You're the expert. Why don't you go and talk to Whit about it? He's back in his study."

"All right, Miz Meade." Again Aaron's mouth lifted. He was walking firmly as he left the room. The trembling seemed to be gone.

Grace looked after him. Her eyes were soft. "Ellie, he does have pride," she said in a low voice. "It's important to him to do the job well. That means something, I think."

Ellie pushed up from her chair. "He does seem to know what he's doing," she said. "Well, I could sit around all day and watch you and Aaron work, but tomorrow's Christmas. I'd better go on and get something done myself."

She pulled her coat on. "Betsy," she called. "Keith. Let's go."

"Aw, do we have to?" Keith complained from the next room. "We're playing!"

"Oh, just let them stay," Grace urged. "You know I love having them. And so does Aaron. I'll send them home in time for dinner."

Ellie hesitated. "I guess they are having fun . . ."

"Of course," Grace assured her. "It's all right, kids. You may stay."

Ellie walked slowly across the street, her hands jammed tight in her pockets. A bleak gray sky hung over the earth that echoed its grayness. The angular trees were gray. The yards were dead gray grass. The gray leaves drifting desolately down sidewalks were pushed along by gusts of wind that would, if she could see them, certainly be gray. Even the little box-houses were drained of the bravery of their colors, and sat closed and gray at the ends of their neat gravel driveways.

She thought about Aaron, and felt empty and tired. Grace had looked at Aaron tenderly, the way a mother looks at a baby. Had Aaron ever known tenderness before?

In her quiet house she stopped. There stood the Christmas tree John had brought home. Still trimmed only with the blue-edged white star he had wired to the highest tuft of needles.

In the kitchen the breakfast plates, sticky with egg, sat on the table. A puddle of chocolate milk spread out around an overturned cup.

She wandered down the narrow hallway, staring through doors. Unmade beds, blankets in a tangle. A hardened peanut butter sandwich on Keith's pillow. A tube of toothpaste on the bathroom floor, mashed, toothpaste worming out from it onto the tiles.

She went back to the kitchen and started a list:
tree
turkey stuffing
make pie

36

How did they all learn to care so much? Is caring something you can learn?

wrap presents

She scratched out *make pie* and wrote *ice cream* underneath. She heated the coffee on the stove, poured a cupful and sipped at it. It tasted stale. She found a bottle of bourbon in the cabinet and added a little to the coffee. She carried the cup to the window and drank slowly, looking out at the stark tree branches. Better put the liquor in the attic before Aaron comes over.

Listlessly, she cleared the table and began to straighten the disordered rooms. Aimless pictures drifted through her brain.

Eyes.

Her mother's eyes, always watching, never at peace, swollen with tears shed and unshed. Her father's eyes, with the fat angry vein that throbbed above them. Eyes in silence, forever accusing the world and her mother and certainly her of some uncommitted crime.

But they're far away now, both father and mother, dead. There can be no more accusation from them.

Then Grace's eyes, comforting.

John's eyes, in tenderness or pity or passion, looking at her. John's eyes.

When Keith and Betsy burst through the door, hungry and shouting, she was just vacuuming the rug. She had not trimmed the tree yet, nor wrapped the presents.

She stuck the vacuum cleaner away in the closet, broiled some hamburgers and opened a can of beans. She sat at the table while they ate, looking at them, not seeing them, answering their excited Christmas talk, not hearing the words of it.

John leaned in through the back door as she was stacking dirty dishes in the sink.

"Ellie," he called, "I'll grab a bite at Whit's if it won't matter to you. I went out after work and got some information about this place Aaron's going to. I'd like to let Whit have a look at what I found out."

"Fine, hon." Ellie forced into her voice a life she didn't feel. "Just hamburgers tonight, anyway."

When the door had closed behind him she turned to the stove where their hamburgers waited, juice slowly congealing. She put them in the refrigerator and fixed herself a cheese sandwich.

Keith darted by, chasing Betsy through the kitchen and down the hall. "Mine! Mine!" His furious yell slammed on Ellie's eardrums.

"Had it first!"

"Ow!"

A crack, soaring wails. Betsy hurled herself into Ellie's legs. "Keith hit me!" she sobbed.

Ellie sighed. "Show me where to put the kiss," she said mechanically. "Keith, come here."

Keith came slowly, his eyes too straightforward, his mouth too carefully expressionless. "She bit me, Mama," he explained virtuously. "Right there, see?" He held out a grimy arm on which a row of small marks was purpling.

He rubbed the arm. "She had my monster model," he said. The blank expression was beginning to break apart around the lip and forehead. "She just took it and all I wanted was I wanted it back before she broke it and the last time I made a model she broke it that very same night before the glue had even got all the way dry and I don't get anything she doesn't wreck and . . ."

"Oh all right, Keith." Ellie felt defeated. "Go do something else, both of you. Now." She gave them each a small shove away from her.

They trailed off, Betsy still sniffling. In a moment another

38

scream pierced in from the living room. Ellie leaned her arms on the sticky edge of the sink, burying her face in them.

Too tired.

She straightened slowly and went to the living room. Betsy crouched under the coffee table, staring watchfully at her brother. Keith sat upright on the couch, turning the pages of a magazine in towering unconcern. Ellie took Keith by the wrist, tugged Betsy up, and propelled them both ahead of her into the bathroom. Without speaking she started water running in the tub and undid Betsy's overalls.

"Mama! Do my buttons too!" Keith shouted over the roar from the faucet.

"Nonsense," Ellie told him. "You're six. Six-year-olds don't need help with buttons."

Keith began to howl. "You always do everything for Betsy. You don't ever help me!"

Ellie looked at him as at a stranger. His whole face seemed to open up when he cried. She heaved Betsy into the water. Then she undid Keith's shirt.

Just get them to bed now. Do the right things some other time.

In the tub Keith whipped up violent waves with his arms and legs. "Hey Betsy," he yelled. "You know what happens tonight Santa Claus comes tonight that's what happens!"

Betsy bounced in the water. "Santa Claus!" she squealed. "Santa Claus! Bring me presents!"

"Mama, can I stay up and see Santa Claus tonight?" asked Keith. "Please?"

"No," Ellie said shortly.

Keith let his waves subside. "I'll do it anyway," he muttered. "I'll come out when you're asleep and stay up all night. I will." He scowled sideways at his mother.

"Presents, presents, presents," Betsy was chanting happily. "Santa Claus bring me presents." She looked at Keith in the other end of the tub. "I want a tail like Keith has," she announced. "Santa Claus bring me tail, Mama? Like that?" She reacher a forefinger toward her naked brother.

"That's not a tail," Ellie began, "that's . . . oh never mind." She plucked Betsy, dripping, out of the tub and swathed her in a towel.

Somehow the pajamas were on, the teeth were brushed.

Ellie stood in Betsy's room and looked at them—Betsy in the youth bed clutching her ragged elephant, Keith a drowsy mound on the folding cot.

No energy left to tell them the Christmas stories. No energy to talk to them, even, or listen to them. They needed so much . . .

She had nothing in her at all to give.

She kissed each one on the forehead and went back to the living room.

She was lying on the couch staring at the bare tree when Grace poked her head through the door. Grace still wore her apron, and there was a smear of ivory paint on one cheek. "Ellie, I'm exhausted," she said. She let the door fall shut and dropped into the easy chair, kicking off her shoes. "I wish we'd thought of some other job for poor Aaron. I wish it didn't have to be my kitchen the day before Christmas!"

"Is it a wreck?" Ellie asked. "I'll fix you a drink." She pulled up from the couch and went to the kitchen.

"A wreck!" Grace called after her. "He did all the woodwork, you know—baseboards, window frames, cupboard doors and shelves, back door, basement door . . . I couldn't get in there all afternoon. Then when he finally got through he just left everything where it was and Whit and John took him downtown again. They're trying to get more paint for the job here tomorrow."

She reached out for one of the glasses Ellie had brought. "Thanks."

"That was a lot of painting for one afternoon," Ellie said. She curled back on the couch.

"Oh, Aaron's fast," said Grace. "And he is good. My kitchen looks better than it has since we bought the house. Even feeling the way he does he did all that work. Whit's been putting it off for three years."

"Whit's had a lot on his mind, hasn't he, with the library?" For some reason Ellie felt defensive.

"Oh yes," Grace admitted. "Whit works hard. But the suffering Aaron goes through every day of his life! And working in spite of it. Whit thinks he knows what that would be like, but he doesn't. Not really. He was never a real alcoholic. But—oh, I don't know . . ." She shook the ice around in her glass, her big eyes puzzled. "Sometimes I think Whit is almost proud of that bad time of his. But that can't be, can it?"

Then she shook her head and sighed deeply. "Ellie, you should see the mess in that kitchen, though. Everything out of the cupboards, everything pulled away from the walls, all the things from dinner left around and nowhere to put them. It's what I call a 'staring mess'—you know, you can't really do anything about it, all you can do is stand there and stare at it. So I left it and came over here."

She took another sip from her glass. "This does help," she said gratefully.

"I was just thinking we'd better put all this up in the attic, with Aaron coming here tonight," Ellie said.

"Oh my, yes," Grace agreed. "Ours is all hidden away. I don't think either of us ought to let him know we have any. It would make the waiting so much harder."

She poked a stray bit of hair back into its sculptured pile. "You know, I really don't mind about the kitchen," she said. "Just think about that poor man, Ellie. He's driven. That's the only word for it. Driven. I haven't anything to complain about."

She sat quietly in the big chair and finished her drink. Then she twisted her feet back into the shoes and stood up. "Well," she said, "I guess I'd better go on back and clean up what I can."

She yawned, patting her mouth with a plump hand. "You're giving Aaron Keith's room?"

Ellie nodded.

"All right, then. Please—do let me know if you need help with anything and I'll be right over."

Again Ellie nodded and followed her to the door.

Then she turned and looked around the room. The couch, with its small bright pillows, the comfortable sagging brown easy chair. Betsy's stuffed clown in its striped suit, sprawled on the rug. A cluster of many-colored crayons sprinkling the coffee table. The Christmas tree, a graceful sweep of deep-green needles, breathing fragrance from its corner.

Poor Aaron Sloane.

She carried the empty glasses to the kitchen. She filled the coffee pot and set it on the stove to brew. The kitchen seemed good now, with the warm coffee smell. A place where people could be alive.

She hurried back to string the lights on the Christmas tree.

When John came in, followed silently by Aaron Sloane, the tree was bright with shining bulbs. The little lights threw glints of red and blue and yellow and green onto hanging glass balls, called answering brightness from the tinsel that twisted from each branch. Ellie got up from the presents she was wrapping and kissed John.

He brushed his lips briefly over her cheek and moved his head toward Aaron. "Aaron's pretty tired, El," he said. "Keith's room ready for him?"

"Of course." Ellie smiled at Aaron, who stood near the door looking down at his worn, polished shoes. "It's in here, Aaron."

42

She led him through the hall, talking cheerfully. "This is where you'll sleep—I think you'll find it's a comfortable bed—here are some of John's pajamas, and the bathroom is over there—oh, I'll put out a towel and washcloth for you . . ."

"Thank you, Miz Clark." Aaron's voice was lifeless. "I'll go on to bed now, if you don't mind." He went into Keith's room and shut the door.

Ellie followed John to their own bedroom. She watched him sit heavily on the bed and untie his shoes. "How's it going, honey?" she asked him.

"Oh, all right, I guess." He stood up and yawned hugely as he unbuttoned his shirt. "That guy's so damn pathetic. Sometimes I think he must be easier to take when he's plastered."

He let his pants crumple to the floor and sat down again, rubbing his insteps. "He's so scared of not doing a perfect job with that painting. It really means something to him to show us how well he can do. We must have gone all over town tonight looking for exactly the right kind of paint for our house trim. Christmas Eve—not many places were open, even the ones that usually stay open in the evening. Grant's was closed, Sears was closed—Pollock's Hardware was open and they had a brand the clerk said was even better, but Aaron didn't want it. Finally we got to some big drugstore in that new shopping center way to hell and gone south of town. They had what he was looking for. Thank God."

He rubbed a hand across his forehead, making black hairs spring up from his eyebrows. "It's expensive paint, costs a lot more than what we used before. But I suppose it's worth it. Of course it's worth it to Aaron."

"Well, a man's pride ought to be worth a few extra dollars," Ellie said. "John, did the tree look all right to you? I got it finished while you were gone."

"Uh-huh." John shifted to his side of the bed and dragged

43

the covers over himself. "I'm just shot, El. Goodnight." He turned on his side, threw an arm over his face, and was closed away from her.

A sudden hotness beat behind her eyes. She marched back to the kitchen and scrubbed and rinsed the soaking dishes with quick, angry movements.

Oh, what do you have to be angry about, Ellie Clark? He's tired. Of course he's tired. He's worked half the night trying to help a man who really needs it. So what's your complaint?

She let the water out, squeezed the sponge and threw it on the counter, and went in to bed.

FOUR

"MAMA! MAMA! DADDY!"

Keith's voice sliced into Ellie's brain, dredging her from sleep.

"Mama! Is it late enough now? Can we be up now? Please? Mama! Daddy!"

Ellie struggled for the unremembered dream. The mattress lurched under Keith's bouncing.

"Daddy? Okay? It's light now and you said when it was light!"

"Uh," John mumbled. "Light. Yes. Minute, Keith." He turned and stretched and groaned.

Ellie lifted heavy eyelids. The window framed a square of pale gray sky, fractured by the maple tree's bare twigs. Keith's face hung over her, white and circular and anxious. His hair stood out in all directions like a bottle brush.

"Can I wake up Betsy now?" he pleaded. "Okay, Mama?"

Ellie rubbed her face. "All right, Keith," she told him. Go get her. We'll be right there." She shoved the covers back and pushed her legs over the side of the bed.

Christmas Day. As she came awake the icicle darts of excitement from childhood Christmases began inside her.

Christmas Day. The words were magic. Christmas Day. A spell, a promise. Lying in bed in the night's darkness, knowing this time Christmas Day would never be. Things that were too good could not really happen. Waking then in the dim early morning, cold with hope and unbelief. Santa Claus and the Christ Child and painted angels with movie star lips. All mixed together. Beautiful, magic, impossible.

Yet, when she dared to look, there the tree would be, there presents would have appeared—proof of all good magic. Proof that even too-much-wished-for things could happen; proof, probably, that life was not what it seemed to be, but some other, lovelier way.

Now, feeling as much a child as Keith, she got up and started for the bedroom door.

John's voice stopped her. "Ellie, put your bathrobe on, for God's sake," he said.

She looked down at the sheer nightgown that shadowed the peaks of her small breasts and fell lightly to the middle of her thighs. "Oh it's not cold in the house," she answered him.

Then, like a smear across the Christmas morning, she remembered Aaron Sloane. She fumbled in the closet for a robe, found the red flannel one, and tied it on securely. John pulled a pair of pants over his pajamas and went ahead of her.

Ellie waited in Betsy's doorway. Keith jumped up and down by the youth bed, jerking at the covers. Betsy turned and mumbled and then was instantly awake.

"Christmas?" she asked. "Santa Claus come?" She crawled backwards out of the bed and chased Keith down the hall. When she ran her bottom wagged like a duck's tail inside the yellow pajamas.

Ellie followed close behind the two of them. The Christmas magic was coming back.

The living room, in spite of all, was just what it ought to be on Christmas. The air held a moist and gently breathing tang of pine. Tree lights spread their colors through the morning dimness, over the mysterious shrouded shapes beneath the branches. Two bulging small socks were taped to the edge of the window-sill. John must have remembered in the night, and put them there.

Keith and Betsy stopped still in the middle of the room, staring huge-eyed. John grinned, watching them from the easy chair. He leaned to Keith and touched his shoulder. "Why do you suppose those socks bump out that way?" he asked.

Keith bounced into life. With a yell he dived for the socks and tugged down the bigger one. Betsy darted for her own. John laughed.

"Maybe that'll hold them long enough for you and me to get some coffee in us," he said.

Ellie raced to the kitchen, the red bathrobe clutching around her ankles as she ran. Hurriedly she filled the coffee pot, set it on the stove, and measured out the coffee. When Aaron's level voice sounded behind her she jumped.

"That coffee'll go good, Miz Clark," he said.

A weight settled to the bottom of her stomach. Again, so soon, she had forgotten he was in their house.

"Why good morning, Aaron," she said. "Merry Christmas."

He was sitting at the kitchen table, wearing Whit's heavy shirt and the old pants. His eyes, fixed on his folded hands, were threaded with pink.

The children are starting to open their presents," she told him. "We're having our coffee in there. Why don't you come on in?"

"I don't think I will right now, Miz Clark," he said. "I've got the paint all stirred up. Thought I'd start on your trim outside right after breakfast." He looked up, not quite at her. "I might just look in later on, though."

"You could have coffee first if you wanted, Aaron." She glanced toward the living room. She felt confused. "Usually we just have coffee while they open their things . . ." She looked at the veins that stood out disturbingly on the backs of his thin hands.

"You do want to get started, of course," she said. "Would you like eggs, Aaron? Toast?"

"Well, now, yes that would be good, Miz Clark. If it's not too much trouble for you. I don't want to be any trouble for you."

She smiled brightly. "It's no trouble at all. Do you want your eggs fried?"

"Well, boiled, if you wouldn't mind, Miz Clark. Four minutes. I don't suppose you were going to cook any bacon? In the next room the children were chattering and squealing.

"Yes, you can have bacon with it," she told him.

"Bacon sure does give a man strength for working out in the cold," he said. "But I wouldn't want you to go to any trouble for me."

"It's no trouble," Ellie said again.

Firming her lips, she took the eggs and bacon from the refrigerator and set a pan of water on the stove to boil. She opened the package of bacon and laid the strips in a row on the skillet. As she watched the bacon shrivel and bulge she could hear Aaron behind her, scraping back his chair, pacing the kitchen. A match rasped and a dry smoke smell mingled with the bacon's sharpness.

"Hurry it up with that coffee, can't you, El?" John called in.

She poked her head through the door. "Let them go ahead

48

and open things," she said. "I'll be there in just a bit." She got back to the stove in time to turn the bacon.

They never tried to have a real breakfast on Christmas. Just coffee—toast or cereal later on. Keith and Betsy were too excited to eat much, and she and John wanted a share in their excitement.

She listened to the chirping squeals from the next room, the sounds of ripping paper. Damn Aaron and his eggs.

She spread butter on the toast.

Oh, don't be that way, Ellie. Why do you give presents anyway? For the children? Or so you can be important because you gave them? Keith and Betsy are all right—give something to somebody who needs it, for a change.

She glanced back at Aaron, striding from window to door behind her. Care about him. Everybody else does.

She forked bacon onto a plate, scooped the eggs from their shells and arranged the toast beside them, poured a cup of coffee.

Aaron slid into his chair stubbing his cigarette into the overflowing ashtray. As Ellie set down the food she peered at him from the safety of her lowered face. His hair was rumpled this morning, uncombed. Lines cut deep between his sunken cheeks and the thin nose that was almost delicate somehow, with lightly flared nostrils. His skin was so white. Prison-white.

He sat at her table, bent over her food. But he didn't belong there. He didn't belong in this house that was for her and her husband and their children. She shivered.

Care about him. She flashed him the too-bright smile. "Have all you want, Aaron," she told him. "There's more of everything. I'll be right in the other room."

He nodded, his mouth moving steadily, full of egg.

Ellie poured coffee for John and herself and escaped to the living room.

The small room was crowded now with open boxes and shreds of ribbon and scattered treasures. Keith squatted in front of the tree, ripping paper from a large package. His face was damp and intent. Betsy hopped about, kicking up bright crumples of wrapping paper, cuddling to her chest a baby doll with rooted hair and pouting lips, crooning to it gently.

John sat cross-legged on the floor. His unlit pipe pushed down the corner of his mouth. He reached gratefully for his coffee when Ellie brought it in. "What took you so long?" he wanted to know.

Ellie got down on the floor beside him. "Aaron wanted breakfast. I guess he needs it, poor man. He's so thin. I fixed him some bacon and eggs."

"He told us he doesn't eat at all when he's drinking," said John, "and not much when he's in those hard-working spells. It's a wonder he's as healthy as he is, maybe."

Once more the fear stabbed in Ellie's mind. As healthy as he is? That cough. Something Keith and Betsy could catch? Tuberculosis or something?

Nonsense.

Determinedly, she took a long drink of coffee, feeling the heat as it slid down her throat. There were a thousand other things a cough might be. Anybody would cough if he smoked as much as Aaron did. Don't look for things to worry about.

Betsy danced over to her, holding a thin lumpy package. "Open it, Mama," she ordered. "Present. I make it."

The package was wrapped in green paper, sealed with strip over strip of tape. Ellie pulled the paper off. Inside was a sheet of drawing paper, folded at odd angles. She unfolded it carefully. It was a large drawing, all in red crayon. The big lopsided circle must be a head—lines were laid over the top for hair. There were two tiny circle eyes, close together, an open grinning mouth showing a triangle of tongue, and no nose. Arms and legs snaked out threadlike from the head.

50

Betsy was hugging herself. "Picture of Mama," she explained delightedly. "I make Daddy a picture of Daddy."

"She did," John said. He found his picture among the things beside him and held it up. It was like the Mama picture, but done in brown crayon. An oblong shape that might have been a pipe, stuck out of the mouth.

Ellie pulled Betsy close. Her small body felt warm and solid, and she smelled of peppermint. "I love the picture, Betsy," Ellie told her. "Thank you."

Keith climbed to his feet, letting a shower of tiny red and white plastic bricks clatter from his lap. "There's another present for you here, Mama," he said. He felt through the papers lying under the tree and handed Ellie a square of folded aluminum foil with an envelope taped to the front. He shifted from foot to foot while she opened the envelope.

"I'll bet you're excited, aren't you, Mama? Can't you not hardly wait to see what it is?" His smile widened over the tooth-swoollen bare pink gums.

The envelope held a piece of red construction paper. A green paper Christmas tree was pasted to it, and the words "Merry Christmas and Happy New Year" were printed in big, careful block letters. Underneath the name "Keith C." trailed in chicken-tracks uphill.

"It's beautiful, Keith," said Ellie. She unfolded the foil, finding inside the square of cardboard with the small calendar pasted to it. Above the calendar was a picture of a yellow and orange striped animal, crouching with claws uplifted. It had five enormous eyes. A row of menacing red-tipped fangs jutted from its mouth.

"It's the Five-Eyed Monster from Mars," Keith said proudly. "He's just finished eating up a whole city-full of people and that's their blood all over his teeth. Mrs. Stewart said we could draw anything we wanted to."

51

"Isn't anybody going to come and slay him?" John wanted to know.

Keith looked thoughtful. "Pretty soon somebody will, I guess. They'll have to drop a hydrogen bomb on him. That's the only way you can get rid of Five-Eyed Monsters."

"He's remarkable," said Ellie. "I'll love having him up on the kitchen wall."

There was a low cough in the doorway. "Mr. Clark." Aaron's voice was soft. The corner of his mouth was raised. "I've got something here for your girl and boy."

He pulled two small packages from a paint-stained pocket. The wrapping rustled in his hands. Keith and Betsy lifted their heads at the sound, expectant. Aaron squatted down, holding out the packages.

"Here, little girl," he said. "Come here, sonny. These are for you."

The children scrambled up and took two more presents, on this day of many presents, from his hands. Impatiently they clawed the paper off, letting it fall to join the other litter on the rug.

There were the boats Aaron had made. Battleships, small, perfect, with smokestacks and guns bristling out. Keith's was painted red and Betsy's yellow. Keith turned his over and over, studying the intricate work.

"Boat!" Betsy squealed happily. "Mine! I like it!"

"I believe Aaron made these himself, kids," John put in. "Didn't you, Aaron?"

"Yes, Mr. Clark." There was pride in Aaron's voice. "I used to do a lot of carving. Got real good at it."

He sat back on his heels. His eyes followed the battleships as the children carried them around. Both corners of his mouth twitched up in more of a smile than Ellie had seen him give before.

"Aaron, they're just wonderful," she said.

52

"I can carve real good," Aaron acknowledged. He got to his feet. "Mr. Clark, would you mind coming outside a minute to see if this trim is the way you want it?"

"All right, Aaron." John used the edge of the chair to help himself up from the floor. "You got an early start today, didn't you?"

"I want to do you a good job, Mr. Clark," Aaron said. "And I have to keep working right along, or I get too nervous."

He turned to Ellie, looking just beyond her. "Maybe you'd like to see it too, Miz Clark." It was not quite a question.

Ellie looked around at Keith and Betsy, scooting their battleships over the rug. "I'd like to, Aaron," she said. "Stay in here, kids, we'll be back in a minute."

Outside Whit's ladder, loaded with rags and different sized brushes, leaned up by the kitchen window. The window frame glistened cleanly white against the brown house siding. Aaron stood looking up at it. "That's a neat job, there," he remarked. Once more his mouth lifted.

"It is," John agreed.

"You ought to have seen it when I did it before, Aaron," Ellie said. She giggled self-consciously. "John and I painted this house ourselves when we first bought it. I got paint all over the glass. It took weeks to scrape it off with a razor blade."

Aaron's mouth twitched again. An expression nearing scorn flickered in the watered-blue eyes. "A good painter never has to scrape any paint off a window." He gestured across the length of the sill. "Look how straight those strokes are."

Ellie's fists squeezed tight in the pockets of the red robe. She'd only meant to make him feel good. The sill had looked all right when she'd done it. Not professional, maybe, but all right.

She watched him with her husband, the two of them looking up at windows, pointing out spots on the guttering, talk-

53

ing intently. She remembered how it had been when she and John had painted the house.

It was the only house they had ever owned, and they had just bought it. Before it there had been a series of one- and two-room apartments, and, after Keith was born, a tiny rented bungalow on a treeless square of yard. Then at last, when Betsy was a baby, there was money enough for a small down payment.

It wasn't a large house, or a particularly well-designed one. Just a nondescript square box enclosing nondescript square rooms—living room, kitchen, one fairly large bedroom for John and Ellie, two smaller ones for the children, and a white-tiled bathroom. The outside was a dingy yellow.

But the house sat back on a deep grassy yard in a neighborhood of deep grassy yards near the edge of town. In front, just outside their bedroom window, the old maple tree flung its beauty wide. And along the sidewalk someone, surely not the same one who painted the house its sickly yellow, had planted a bittersweet vine to grow in a brilliant tumble of winter-orange berries over a single split rail of fence.

John and Ellie had done the painting right away—before the last of the boxes was unpacked, before the furniture was arranged, before the curtains were up. They had done it themselves because it cost so much to have it done.

For weeks they had lived in a confusion of sticky ladders and wet-handled brushes. For weeks the clean sharp smell of paint had been in everything they touched or wore, the taste of it in the food they ate.

Keith had been as square and as unstoppable as a truck, peering into cans and falling off step stools and trailing paint wherever he went. Betsy had looked on, fat and serious and enchanted, from her playpen under the maple tree.

Then finally the house had stood gleaming on its lawn behind the bittersweet and the October-bright maple. Choco-

54

late-brown siding, crisp ivory trim. Unexpectedly, a door of fiery orange-red—John's idea.

And then the house had been truly theirs.

Ellie scowled at Aaron's back as he looked up proudly at the new paint spread so expertly over her paint. For a moment she let herself hate every crease in his scrawny neck.

John clapped him on the shoulder. "Well, it looks just great," he said heartily. "We're lucky to have you here."

He started toward the door. "I guess it's time to get ready for church—want to come with us, Aaron?"

"No, I think I won't, Mr. Clark," said Aaron politely. "I think I'll just stay and get your trim finished up for you."

He moved the ladder to the next window, set his paint can on it, and climbed up.

John nodded and went back into the house. Ellie, shivering now in her thin robe, ran after him.

A shrill tide of wailing met them from the living room. Keith, his cheeks ballooned and flaming, lay stomach-down over a toy wheelbarrow, clinging to it possessively. Betsy sat astride him and howled. Her eyes were squeezed shut and she was pounding his back with furious fists.

"Betsy!" John snapped. "Keith!" He pulled Betsy up and slapped her bottom, pushing her over to Ellie. Then he dragged Keith from the wheelbarrow and slapped him, too. "Get along there, both of you," he ordered. "It's late."

Ellie took them and rushed them through their dressing, hurried them through bowls of cornflakes. Dressed, somehow, herself.

Christmas Day. Magic. But when the magic ends, for magic always ends, how hard returning to a world unchanged and a life that is no more than it has ever been.

Aaron didn't look around when the Plymouth's motor started behind him. He stood on the ladder drawing his brush easily down the side of another window frame. No tremor shook his hand now.

Ellie was still stabbing bobby pins into her hair. "John, do you think it's all right to leave him?" she whispered.

John threw the car into gear and twisted his head to see out the back window. "All right?" he demanded. "What do you mean? Keith, sit down, can't see through you."

"Do you think it's all right to let him stay here alone? He's so . . ." Ellie groped for a word that might explain her fear.

John looked over at her. His eyebrows pulled together. "Aaron's not going to steal the silverware, Ellie," he said. "The poor guy is painting our house. He's like a kid. Didn't you see how badly he needed us to like his work? Didn't you see how he needs to be liked himself? All he wants now is a chance to show us he's grateful."

He backed the car out of the driveway and onto the black-paved street. "Maybe you should have stayed at Whit's house with us the other night—when he opened up and started talking about himself. Aaron's not anything to be afraid of, Ellie."

He swung the Plymouth around a corner and the house was out of sight. "Didn't you see how he looked when he gave Keith and Betsy those boats he'd made? He didn't come in till everything else was opened—maybe he was afraid the kids wouldn't notice his presents."

"He just wants to show off everything he does," Ellie said softly, and at once was sorry she had said it.

John frowned at the street ahead. "Listen, Ellie," he said sternly, "I know it's not another Christmas present to have him here, but he's unhappy and confused and afraid. He's a lot like a little kid who's unhappy, I think. You might stop and remember what Christmas is supposed to be all about. Or what

56

it used to be about before it got turned into Santa Claus and expensive toys and damn little else."

Ellie sat rigid on her seat. John was right. Why did he have to be right and throw his rightness at her? Why did she always have to make him mad?

FIVE

ELLIE SAT NEXT TO JOHN IN THE DIM CHURCH, NOT THINKING, letting the place wash over her like an ocean. Stained-glass light patching carved arches, dark pews. Sacramental smell of burning beeswax and polished wood and mildew. Organ chords marching in majestic procession down the aisles, trembling among silence in the corners. Words . . . sonorous words, well-learned; their meanings drowned in familiarity.

She knew that someday she would have to think about all this—really think about it. God . . . life . . . what the meanings are . . .

There were times when she began to think too much and was afraid, when she feared both the possibility of God and the possibility of a world without God. Sometimes nothing else but God made any sense at all. And yet once in a while the idea came sliding to the rim of her mind that all this—the religion that had been handed her—seemed to make too much sense . . . a story with too pat an ending, every loose end tucked too neatly in place, no dangling awkward questions. And Ellie did have questions.

But she did not ask them now. Enough to sit still and let

58

the old words wash about her; gentle, familiar, two thousand years old.

". . . and the angel said to them: Fear not; for, behold, I bring you good tidings of great joy that shall be to all the people . . ."

Words of safety, of stomach-warmth, if you just hear them, with no thinking.

The music rose and surged viscerally through her, and she merged her voice with all the voices, with centuries of voices that understood, perhaps, more deeply than she: "O Come, all ye faithful, joyful and triumphant . . ."

She left John's side and worked against the crowd to the nursery where Keith and Betsy were. When she reached the front steps of the church again, with the children racing around her, a sharp-beaked woman in a pink coat was talking to John; holding him fast with a white-gloved hand and a fierce bright glare.

Claire Holman. Ellie sighed. This could take a while.

Mrs. Holman swung around when she saw Ellie and drew her in with the other white glove. "Ellie, my dear," she crowed, "I saw your house being painted when we drove by this morning. I was so surprised, it being Christmas and all, and John has just told me about your—guest, would you call him? I do have to tell you one thing about alcoholics, my dears, and I am speaking from experience." Her glare darted from Ellie back to John. "With alcoholics, expect failure. That is all I can tell you. Expect failure."

She nodded triumphantly. Blue-white ringlets jiggled under her hat. "My first husband was an alcoholic. Died of it. I know alcoholics. Ralph there," she beamed at the tired-looking man standing quietly, apart from them, "has never touched a drop. Expect failure with an alcoholic. Always."

She released John to clutch at an angular, long-faced woman who had been edging around their group on the steps.

"Here's Wilma Kirkland—Wilma, John and Ellie are taking care of an alcoholic—John tells me the man is living with them. You remember Robert, don't you, Wilma? My first husband, Robert?

Wilma Kirkland's narrow features sorted themselves into a sympathetic grimace. "Oh yes," she said. "I remember Robert well."

"Robert was still alive when we moved to Rockfield." Mrs. Holman shook her head sadly. "It was the next year that he died. Nineteen-forty-seven. February, nineteen-forty-seven. It was his liver. From drinking." The ringlets bobbed in emphasis. "The doctors had warned him, and I told him and told him to cut down. 'You'll drink yourself to death, Robert,' I kept saying to him. But he never listened. That's what I've been telling John and Ellie—I've been telling them they must expect failure with an alcoholic."

"Yes. Yes, I suppose you're right." Wilma's face smoothed and brightened. "Look, Claire, I've got to run. I'm expecting my sister's boy down from Chicago this afternoon, and I'm having a big Christmas dinner for him. He's spending the holidays with us." She turned a wide tooth-filled smile to Ellie. "Pleased to see you, Ellie. And John. Beautiful service, wasn't it? And you must meet Byron . . . well, he'll be staying through New Year's, of course. Good luck with your alcoholic." She hurried off.

"Goodbye," Ellie called after her.

Your alcoholic.

"Remember to expect failure," Mrs. Holman reminded them brightly.

John's smile looked nailed to his face. "I appreciate your interest," he said. "We'd better get home now. It's been a long morning for the kids." He propelled Betsy and Keith into the car.

Ellie followed. Your alcoholic.

60

John settled behind the steering wheel and pulled his pipe out of his overcoat pocket. "Good God," he said. "I wonder how much of that kind of thing Aaron has to put up with? Poor guy."

"Poor Aaron." Ellie put her hat on the seat beside her and leaned back, closing her eyes while John drove. She didn't open them until the Plymouth stopped in their driveway.

Aaron was sitting on the ladder, smoking jerkily. His shoulders—terribly thin shoulders—dropped forward. His chest was hollow under Whit's old shirt. All the muscles of his face sagged, and his eyes stared mistily at nothing. The paint cans stood abandoned around the base of the ladder.

"John, he wasn't like that when we left," Ellie whispered.

John jumped out of the car. "Aaron?" he said. "You feeling bad, man? Come in and have some coffee."

Aaron moved his head in a dejected arc that covered the cans and the brushes and the half-painted frame of the picture window. "I didn't finish with your trim yet, Mr. Clark," he said. "I'm sorry." Ellie could hardly hear him.

He stepped heavily down from the ladder, hunching his shoulders more protectively, and trailed into the house. He sat in the kitchen, on the chair John pulled out for him. He rested his face in his hands. His palms dug into his closed eyes. When Betsy and Keith buffeted his chair on their frantic race to their presents, he didn't move.

Alarmed, Ellie watched him from the door.

"Coffee, Ellie," John reminded her. "And how about a few sandwiches?"

She roused herself and turned on the burner under the coffee pot; found a loaf of bread and some cold meat.

John sat next to Aaron. He undid his overcoat with one hand, leaving it on. "Any way I can help, Aaron?" he asked.

Aaron slid his hands down his gaunt cheeks. "I don't know

if I can make it, Mr. Clark. You've all been so good to me. But I don't know."

He shook his head slowly. "Maybe you just better give me the money for what I've done so far and let me stop bothering you. I've been nothing but bother to you."

John looked hard into Aaron's eyes, as if he could force them to meet his. "You can make it, Aaron," he said urgently. "I know you can. It won't be so long now."

Aaron shook his head again. His voice was almost a whisper. "I don't know, Mr. Clark. Feel like I've got to get away. Maybe if I could get away for just a little while first then I wouldn't mind that hospital place so bad."

He pulled a mashed pack of cigarettes from his shirt pocket. He clawed a cigarette out, got it into his mouth. He bent his head to a match that shook in his cupped hands.

"I really think you'd better stay with us, Aaron," John said. "We'll all help you. You won't be alone."

Aaron flipped out the match and dropped it into the ashtray. His eyelids, shut against the smoke, were a crumpled purple-white. He stood up and shuffled away from them into the hall. Then he turned and came back to the kitchen. He stopped beside Ellie at the sink and cleared his throat thickly.

"Miz Clark," he said, "I just wondered . . . would you mind . . . do you know how to shorten pants?"

"Shorten pants?" Ellie was startled.

Aaron looked at her face, somewhere below her eyes. "Those pants they gave me at the prison are too long," he said. "I don't want to bother you any more, Miz Clark. But I do hate to wear them to that hospital the way they are. They don't look right. It sure would be good of you to turn them up for me, if you have the time. Only I wouldn't want it to be any trouble for you."

Ellie felt helpless, foolish. Cuffs were hard to make. She couldn't do it right. Once she had tried to shorten a new

62

pair of pants for John—she had thought she could save him the price of having it done at the store and he would be proud of her. It had taken a long time, a dismally long time, and it had been hard. She had turned and stitched and ripped out and turned and stitched again, and when she had finished at last she had been hot and trembling and ready to cry. The pants had looked all wrong, with an extra fold coming somehow through the center of each cuff, making them lumpy. John hadn't said anything about it, but she had been ashamed.

"I've . . . I've never made cuffs, Aaron," she said. "I'm not sure I'd know how to do it."

"They don't need to be a lot shorter, Miz Clark," Aaron said. "Only about an inch. Maybe you wouldn't mind just trying? I'll get them and show you." He went back down the hall to Keith's room.

Ellie looked at John, pleading. "John, I can't do cuffs," she said.

"Oh, it's not that big a job, El." He sounded disgusted, she thought. "Just look at the old cuffs before you rip them out. You'll see how they ought to go." He lowered his voice. "Can't you see how much it means to Aaron right now?"

She felt caught in a trap.

"Well, I'll try," she said without much hope. "I'd better get the turkey in first, though, if it's going to be done by evening."

She threw open the refrigerator door and brought out the turkey in its foil wrapping—all stuffed since yesterday, thank heaven. She put it in the roasting pan and shoved it into the oven.

"That all?" John asked.

"That's all for now," she said.

"How can it be so quick?" he wanted to know. "Grace has been cooking for days."

"The sweet potatoes are canned," she said defensively.

63

"The peas and cranberry sauce are canned. The rolls are brown-an-serve. Ice cream for dessert."

Grace doesn't have a job, she told herself. Grace doesn't have children. Tears stung behind her eyes. Furiously she held them back.

Grace doesn't go around feeling sorry for herself all the time.

"There's the plate of sandwiches on the table," she said.

She went to get her sewing basket and met Aaron coming out of Keith's room. Hanging over his arm was the pair of pants he had worn when she first saw him. It was folded neatly, with creases together and seams pulled straight.

"Here's what I mean, Miz Clark," he said. "Your little boy got me some pins." He folded back one pants leg without disturbing the crease. "You see, I put them in along here." He ran a white finger along the line of pins.

Ellie nodded without speaking. She took the pants from him and her hand touched his. His hand was cold. It felt hard, dried, like something that was long dead or that had never been alive. She thought she could feel the bones beneath the thin tough layer of skin. She walked on into her bedroom, holding the pants out away from her without being aware that she did.

She sat down at her sewing table, stretched out a pants leg, and studied the fold in its cuff. Just relax. Take enough time to do it right. She bent close to her work, holding the layers of cloth tight between her fingers, slipping the needle cautiously from layer to layer.

Aaron walked in, a blurred figure beyond the cuff she stared at. He moved up to her, watched for a moment, moved noiselessly out. Hotness burned behind her eyes.

At last she put her thimble away and stabbed the needle into its cushion. There was an ache of tension between her shoulder blades. She shut her eyes and tiny stitches shone orange, not gray, under their lids.

Then she held the pants out and squinted at them. Not too bad. Not the way a department store tailor would do them, but not bad. Maybe she could even do John's pants.

The crease was gone, of course. She threw the pants over her arm, took them to the kitchen, and pulled out the ironing board.

As she ironed she listened to the sounds from the living room—voices, John's voice, mostly; thumps, giggles from the children; Aaron's wheezy cough.

The turkey radiated its crisp roasting fragrance from the oven. Steam hissed out from the pants as she worked over them, pulling an acrid, sanitary smell into the air.

"Here you are, Aaron," she called at last. She set the iron on its stand.

Aaron came into the kitchen. A stub of cigarette hung ash-heavy from his lip. He picked the pants off the ironing board and squinted at them. Ellie looked over his shoulder. The cuffs were not perfect. The iron had brought each fault into whitened relief.

Aaron tossed his cigarette into the ashtray and ran his thumbs along the cuffs. He rolled the cloth back and forth, roughing out the shine. "Miz Clark," he said, "if you wouldn't mind, could you go over this with your iron one more time? Right here, you see." He tapped a place on the left cuff. "It's not straight there. If it wouldn't be any trouble for you."

He spread the pants on the board again and lit another cigarette.

Ellie's stomach gripped. She straightened the cuff with angry short stabs of the iron. When she whipped the pants off the board her knuckle brushed against the iron. She shoved the pants toward Aaron and turned away from him to suck the burned spot.

"Thank you for your trouble, Miz Clark," he said politely. He gave his half-smile. "I'll have a shower now, if you don't mind, and get dressed. Miz Meade's expecting me." He folded his pants carefully and carried them away with him.

Ellie went to the living room, blowing on her knuckle. Betsy and Keith were wrestling gleefully on the floor, squealing, rolling over and over among scattered toys.

John smiled at her. "I'm glad you did that for him, Ellie," he said. "I've been thinking about him—about the way he tries to be so neat most of the time. It must be terribly important to him to be clean, to have his clothes fit. The way he looks is all in the world he has. Maybe he can only feel that he counts for something—that he's a man, really—when he's well dressed. Clothes would be that important to me, I think, if I didn't have any other way to feel like somebody."

"Mm hmm." Ellie sank down on the couch and felt for a cigarette from the box on the end table. She looked at the Christmas tree. Three of the flame-shaped bulbs had burned out. John offered his lighter. She leaned forward to it and watched the smoke float upward.

Aaron. His neat pants, the clean businessman's shirt. The clothes weren't right, though. Some way, no matter how clean they were, no matter how well they fit, they would never be right. They could never cover enough. You would still see the gaunt defeated face, the hopeless eyes. The clothes might stand and sit and bend, but no man would ever live inside them.

She looked at her watch and put her cigarette out. Time to put on the peas and potatoes, open the cranberry sauce. Thank heaven Aaron was eating with Whit and Grace.

She smiled at John as she got up. But it's like Aaron's clothes, she thought—does it really cover anything when I smile?

None of them had much to say at dinner. The children,

66

tired from all their excitement, picked at the food. Keith mashed a piece of turkey into his cranberry sauce and stirred it around listlessly. "This stuff has skin on it," he observed. "I like chicken better."

Betsy, her plate forgotten, was picking her paper napkin into confetti.

Ellie looked around the table. The dismembered turkey, its stuffing spilling sadly onto the platter. The dull-green and tasteless peas. The cardboard-stiff rolls . . .

John, his face expressionless, steadily forking up meat. Keith and Betsy, their heads bobbing with fatigue.

"It's not exactly like Charles Dickens," Ellie said.

John reached for a roll. "Well, maybe not," he said, "But I guess it's life."

They were finishing the chocolate ice cream when Aaron came out of Keith's room. His crisp black-and-gray hair lay back in wet comb-lines. He had shaved carefully. He wore the spotless shirt and jacket, and the newly fitted gray pants.

"Mr. Clark," he said, "if it's not any trouble, would you have a coat I could borrow to wear to Mr. Meade's house? It's getting some colder, and all I have is this jacket." He stood quietly waiting.

John looked up at him slowly. "Yes, certainly, Aaron," he said. "You can take the brown coat that's in the living room closet."

Aaron nodded and went quietly out of the room. In a moment they heard the front door click shut behind him.

John rubbed his eyelids. "Lord, how I'd hate having to ask somebody for every single thing I needed," he said.

Ellie left the dishes on the table and brought coffee into the living room. Keith had turned on the television set. The room was filled with Christmas music, slowed and stretched and heavy with the rumble of an electric organ—a thick syrup through which the actors moved in some nostalgic scene.

"Oh God," said John. "The shows are all going to be heartwarming tonight, aren't they? That I can do without."

He switched the set off again and leaned back in the big easy chair. Keith scowled briefly when the music stopped, then was absorbed again in his building of plastic bricks. Betsy sat near the tree, her fat legs sticking straight out in front of her, pulling the dress off her new doll.

Ellie curled in her usual spot on the couch. She sipped her coffee, breathed it in. She made herself think about nothing but the coffee—its steam in her nostrils, the sharp-edged cleanness of its taste.

John put down his cup. He stood up and yawned. "I think maybe I'll go over to Whit's," he said. "Aaron looked pretty bad this afternoon. I'm sort of worried about him."

"There's just tonight left, isn't there?" Ellie asked. "You and Whit are taking him to Cedarville in the morning, aren't you?"

"Right." John hunched into his old gray jacket. "But I think tonight's going to be the hardest time for the poor guy. If we can just get him through tonight . . ."

Keith bounced up from his bricks. "I wanna go with you, Daddy!" he shouted. "Grace hasn't seen my new fire truck!"

"Take me too! Me too!" Betsy squealed.

"Okay, kids. Get your coats," said John. He smiled at them, his eyes smiling too, behind the dark-framed glasses.

Ellie watched him. He is good looking, she thought suddenly. He really is. He's good.

John was fitting Betsy's arms into her hooded car coat. "Why don't you come too, El?" he asked her.

"I think I'll stay here," she answered. "Get the kitchen cleaned up—things like that. Maybe I'll come over later if you're there that long."

She watched them cross the street, Keith racing ahead of John, Betsy dancing along beside him. Then she closed the door and went back into the quiet kitchen. It was good to be alone somehow. Good not to have to be anything to anybody.

Why could she never feel like herself when anyone else was there? Even with John she was always acting, it seemed—always pretending to be better, or nicer, or kinder, than she knew she was.

Is it truly so bad, then, whatever hides beneath the pretending?

Suddenly crawling near, the hidden blackness . . . It was a blackness that she felt inside of her, an echoing and unsafe emptiness. Or possibly, frighteningly, not an emptiness, but something more terrible. She, the Ellie Clark people saw, was only a brittle shell above the blackness. If she should let go, fall, break apart . . .

She shivered. She began to scrape the plates, humming feverishly as she worked. ". . . God rest ye merry, gentlemen, let nothing you dismay . . ."

Little by little the blackness receded. She was safe above it once again, and busy, and alone.

The doorbell's peremptory note cut through the clatter of dishes. Surprised, she ran to the door and opened it.

There stood Aaron. His eyes showed rings of white, vein-streaked, around their pale irises. His hair stood up in tufts. A red spot burned high on each protruding cheekbone. He was all by himself.

SIX

"MIZ CLARK."

Aaron's voice was a hoarse whisper. "Miz Clark, would you do something for me?" He stepped over the threshold, his papery eyelids blinking. His fists bunched out the pockets of John's overcoat. The coat was too short. Ellie had never realized before how tall Aaron was.

She flattened against the open door, too aware of the empty house around her. Then she made herself stand easily. *He feels bad, that's all. John said tonight would be his hardest time.* She closed the door. It was as if she forced it shut through mud.

"What is it you want, Aaron?" she asked him. "Where are John and the others?"

"They're all still at the house over there, Miz Clark," he said. "I told them I was tired. Said I'd come back here and go to bed."

He pulled a hand out of his pocket. The white fingers shoved through his hair. "I've got to get away for a while, Miz Clark," he said. "You don't know how bad I feel. I can't take it any more. It's like jail, with them watching me all the time."

He rubbed his crumpled eyelids. "Miz Clark, would you mind just driving me downtown—let me have enough money to see a movie? I've earned it. I'll call you afterward and you can come get me."

"Oh Aaron, I just don't know . . ." What if he doesn't want to see a movie? What if he just wants to go out and get drunk?

"I wouldn't mind so much going to that place if I could get away a while first," he said.

Of course he wants to get drunk, she thought. We're supposed to keep him from getting drunk. Oh why isn't John here?

"I think it would be better if I called my husband first, Aaron, and talked to him about it," she said hesitantly.

She moved backward and reached for the telephone. Time. Time. It's John's job, or Whit's. I can't take care of him.

Aaron stepped close to her. For the first time since she had known him he looked straight at her, the pale-irised eyes thrusting sharply into her eyes. "Don't call your husband, Miz Clark," he said, low, firmly.

Her eyes held by his, she lifted her hand from the receiver. She bit at the side of her thumbnail.

"Don't call him," Aaron repeated. "Your husband makes me feel like I'm in jail when he talks to me the way he does. Just drive me downtown now, Miz Clark. Give me the money I earned. Don't call any of them."

"All right," she said. Her voice seemed not her own. "Get in the car. I'll be there. I'll get my bag."

Do what he wants. She wrenched away from his look and ran to her room. She tugged a scarf from her bureau drawer. He needs to have people trust him, that's it. He needs to be treated like a grown man. She folded the scarf over her smooth bun of hair, tied it beneath her chin. Trust him.

71

But I don't trust him. He can't have money, he can't be on his own. John kept him here before. I don't trust him at all.

Her face in the mirror was white and small. Her eyes looked too big for her face. Had those shadows always been under them? Automatically she ran a pink lipstick over her lips and pressed them together. She grabbed her purse from the bureau and ran through the hall and out of the house, slid into the Plymouth. Don't leave time to be afraid.

Aaron sat on the seat beside her, leaning forward impatiently, jabbing a cigarette into his mouth, jerking it out, puffing bursts of smoke.

Ellie put the car in gear and backed down the driveway. She couldn't look at him. "What theater, Aaron?" she asked.

"I'll tell you where to let me off, Miz Clark," he said. "I'll probably walk around some and see what's playing different places." He smashed his cigarette butt hard into the ashtray. She heard the match scrape as he lit another.

The small car was filling with smoke. Her eyes watered. She rolled her window down, but the dense moist air of the clouded night seemed only colder, as stifling as the smoke. She drove in silence through vacant streets, past closed-up houses bright with Christmas lights. Her hands in their brown wool gloves held tight to the steering wheel.

Beside her, Aaron shifted restlessly. "Miz Clark, your husband sure likes to take over, doesn't he?" The level voice had an intensity Ellie had never heard in it before. "He's a good man, but he's mean, too."

She gripped the wheel still harder. Her face burned. "Is that what you think, Aaron?"

"He's mean," Aaron said. "He wants to keep me like I'm in jail. Him and Mr. Meade. But your husband is more nervous."

She glanced sideways at him. He had turned toward her. His eyes, a luminous green-white in the light from the dash-

72

board, caught hers. Quickly she looked back at the winding road.

"I don't know how a woman like you can live with a man that takes over the way your husband does," he said. He shifted again, a little closer to her, she thought, but she wasn't sure.

She drove steadily, biting her lower lip, fighting the urge to speed. Tonight is his hardest time, John said so. He's a sick man.

Sick man sick man sick man. Her mind jabbered the words senselessly, blotting out the crowding anger, the crowding fear.

The houses along the empty road were giving way to scattered businesses—a small motorcycle shop, a frozen custard place, a filling station or two. Aaron leaned forward as they came near a sagging frame box of a building. A sign over the door said GRILL in sizzling red neon, and then, in smaller letters, BEER.

"Would you mind just stopping there, Miz Clark," he said, pointing.

Mindlessly, she obeyed, and pulled the car onto the littered dirt strip in front of the building. She sat with her hands still on the wheel, staring at the buzzing sign.

You do everything he wants you to do, she thought. He wants you to shorten his pants and you do it, he wants you to drive him downtown and you do it, he wants to go to a beer joint and you take him there. If he wants . . .

"Aaron, you know they won't let you into the alcoholic center if you've had a beer, even," she said in a rush. She glanced over at him. Now his face reflected the red of the neon. The corner of his mouth seemed to lift in its half-smile.

"I left a coat of mine here, Miz Clark," he said calmly. "A good coat. It was before I was in prison this last time. I remember I gave it to the man here to keep for me and I never got it back. I sure would like to have that coat before I go to the alcoholic place."

He reached for the door handle. "You don't have to go in if you don't want, Miz Clark," he said. "I'll be right back." He slipped out of the car and disappeared inside the old building.

Ellie shivered and stuffed her hands into her coat pockets. She looked around. The beer joint sat in a weedy field between two filling stations. The filling stations were both black and silent. Christmas night. Of course.

Would they sell him beer tonight? Well, probably so, here, if he asked for it.

Maybe there really was a coat. Aaron certainly needed it, if there was one. She tried to believe in the coat, but her mind refused the belief.

He'll come back drunk. Or not drunk, maybe—how drunk can you get on beer—but . . .

Why was he talking that way about John? Why did I come with him? What am I doing here alone, waiting? Prison. Nobody ever asked him why it was prison.

He'll come back drunk and I'll be waiting. What if . . .

She pushed her hands over her ears. What could she do if he tried that? Scream. Scream and scream . . .

She pulled her hands down. Nobody would hear. Not out here. Or if he made her stop someplace else. Was there anything in the car? A knife? Or a wrench?

She knocked open the glove compartment and rummaged through it.

No. Nothing. Only maps and a packet of John's pipe tobacco. Sweet, woody-smelling tobacco, smelling like John.

John. She banged the compartment shut again. What could she do? She might hit him with her knee, standing up. But if they were in the car? And Aaron was big. Thin, but so tall. And used to hard work.

74

Maybe nothing would help. She dug her palms hard against her eyes. The blackness swirled up behind the lids. It musn't happen to me. I couldn't stand it.

What if I like it? Oh God what if I like it?

Light poured golden from the door of the building onto packed black dirt. Aaron swung down the two splintery steps and eased into the car.

She pulled tight against her door, watching him. His pale eyes searched hers. This time she was certain he smiled. "It was still there, Ellie," he said.

At the sound of her name, ice shot through her. Then she saw the worn black coat as he laid it carefully over the back of the seat. A smell of rancid beer breathed from the cloth. "Man kept it for me," he said, still looking at her, not at the coat. "Good thing for him he did." His voice neither rose nor fell.

He felt in his pocket and brought out the pack of cigarettes. "Now go on, Ellie," he said. "I'll tell you where to stop next."

Biting her teeth together to keep them still, she fumbled with the key and got the car started. She drove on into the business district, stopping at traffic lights without seeing them, making the turns as Aaron pointed them out. It might have been Aaron's town, and she the stranger in it. Anywhere, she thought, I'll drive you anywhere—only go then and be gone.

Aaron smoked quietly, the half-smile still on his lips.

"You can let me out here," he said at last. She drew the car up to the curb. She looked around. They were at one of the main intersections, a block from the square. Several movie theaters near here. Several bars, most of them open, even on Christmas night.

"Would you give me some money, Ellie?" Aaron asked. He spoke patiently, as one might remind a child.

She opened her purse. So easy. Just give whatever he asks

for. She took out a five-dollar bill and put it into his hand. He nodded approval.

He climbed out of the car, took off John's overcoat, and slid his arms into his own. He stuffed her money into his pocket and dropped the brown coat on the seat of the car. "I'll call you when the movie's over," he said, and strode away down the sidewalk.

She slumped in her seat, drained empty. He was gone. Nothing had happened. She was whole. Untouched.

She rested her forehead on the rim of the steering wheel. Then, angrily, she straightened and shook herself and started the car.

Of course nothing had happened. How stupid to think it would. Like a child in a dark room, pretending bogeymen. She raced the motor and pulled the Plymouth out from the curb. She drove toward home, fast, through Christmas-quiet streets. Store windows were dimly lighted, their seductive treasures abandoned now. Street lights were dripping tinsel. Flashing glimpses of Christmas trees in living rooms.

What makes Aaron Sloane a bogeyman, anyway? Because he was mad at John? Because he smiled at me? Because he called me by my first name, the way everybody else does? She gripped the wheel viciously, hating him.

Aaron Sloane is a sick man, she told herself. He needs friends, he needs help. He's afraid. He must be terribly afraid. Twenty years in jail after jail. Why wouldn't he hate a home that was like a jail? Her hands on the wheel relaxed a little.

Of course he wants a few hours by himself, with nobody watching. Maybe that's all he does want. I'd want that, dreadfully.

Halfway home she thought about John.

John didn't know where she was—she hadn't even left a note. He would be worried if he knew she was gone. John did worry about her. What would he think? What could she tell him when she got home?

John, Aaron asked me to let him off downtown, so I did.

Suddenly, put like that, it was an unthinkable thing she had done. Aaron hadn't ever meant to see a movie. He was downtown, he was on his own, and he had money—plenty of money to start him off. And it was her fault.

Aaron had begged them to take care of him. Probably he knew there would be a time like tonight. He knew he hadn't the strength in himself to wait out three days.

So what happens? The first time I'm called on to give him strength I simply fold.

Tears spurted to her eyes. "Why in God's name did they ever leave me alone with that man?" she shouted irrationally in the lonely car. "They ought to know I couldn't be strong enough for him. It's all I can do to hold myself up! They know that! They know that!"

She drove the familiar streets blindly, sobbing her helpless fury to the unhearing night. "I'm not that strong! Don't they know me?"

She left the car in front of the Meades' house and burst through their door without knocking. John was there still, talking with Grace and Whit in the firelight. Keith and Betsy slept, head to head, on the couch. None of them had even missed her yet.

The startled faces that turned to her shimmered beyond her erupting tears. John jumped up and grabbed her shoulders, searching her face. "Ellie, what is it?" he demanded.

Grace and Whit crowded in. Ellie felt smothered, crushed by questioning eyes. She gulped for air.

"You left me alone," she accused them, sobbing. "You just went off and left me alone, and you know what I'm like, and he came and wanted me to take him out and of course I did. You ought to have known I'd do anything he wanted me to!

You all ought to have!" She clutched at John and hid her face in his shoulder, away from the eyes.

Grace touched her arm. "Are you talking about Aaron?" she asked. "Did he do . . . anything?"

Whit's thin voice was stern. "Ellie," he said. "Tell us. Did Aaron hurt you?"

"Hurt me?" Ellie quieted, turning to look at Whit. "Hurt me? Oh, no, no, for God's sake, no. But he's gone. I let him go and he's gone." She clung tight to John, crying again violently.

John led her to Whit's big chair and made her sit in it. "Now, listen, Ellie," he said firmly, perching on the chair arm, "stop that. Try to tell us what happened."

Ellie leaned against him, gasping, struggling to pull together scattered parts of herself. "Well," she said carefully, "Aaron came to our house—it must have been about seven o'clock . . ."

She looked down at her watch. Only a little after eight. Had it really been so short a time?

"He told us he was tired," Grace put in.

"Well, he wasn't," said Ellie. "He looked wild—it scared me, the way he looked, the way he talked. He told me to drive him downtown so he could see a movie. He said you were all keeping him in jail here and he couldn't stand it any more. He said lots of things. He said he wanted to get out by himself for a few hours before he had to go to the alcoholic center. And he wanted money, for the movie, he said. I was going to call John, but he told me not to. So I didn't. I just took him downtown. He said he'd call when he wanted to come back."

Her eyes swam again with tears. "Only he isn't going to a movie, I know," she said hopelessly. "He has five dollars—I gave it to him—and he's going to get drunk and not get into the center and he'll probably be in jail again and it's my fault. I just wrecked everything you were trying to do." She doubled over with her head on her knees, crying soundlessly.

John gave her an absent pat and stood up. "Well, Whit, I guess he will get drunk," he said.

"He probably will," Whit agreed. "But there is an off-chance he'll be okay. He did tell Ellie he'd call. Maybe we'd better go back to your house to be there if he does. That's all in the world we can do now."

SEVEN

"I SUPPOSE WHIT AND I COULD DRIVE AROUND TOWN," JOHN SUG-
GESTED. "We might happen to see Aaron."

They were waiting in the Clarks' living room. The waiting had gone on forever, it seemed to Ellie. She huddled in
a corner of the couch. The base of her throat was hard with
not crying.

Whit stared thoughtfully at the Christmas tree's blue-
rimmed star. "We could," he said. "But I'm not so sure it
would be a good idea. Might make it seem as if we don't trust
him. If he knew we'd come looking."

"Well, I don't trust him," said John. "But you're right, I
guess." He took his pipe from the coffee table and knocked
out its blackened wad of tobacco.

Grace sat beside Ellie, knitting tan yarn onto a bulky
ribbed square. Her back was propped straight against the
cushions; her smooth rounded legs crossed each other neatly
at the ankles. She frowned, and the rhythm of her needles
faltered.

"Oh I am so worried," she said, not for the first time. "He
just has to come back and let us help him. He can't go through
that whole terrible business again,"

From the easy chair Whit reached over to her and squeezed her wrist gently. "We'll do anything we can, dear," he assured her. "If he calls us we'll take care of him. But you know we can't make him call." His voice went higher. "Grace, you'll have to be prepared for the possibility that he might not call."

"I wish you wouldn't keep saying that," Grace sighed.

She spread the square of wool over her knees. It lay thick and soft on the heavy blue crepe of her dress. She smoothed it out. "His sweater is coming right along," she said. "He does need something good and warm to wear, poor man. He has so little.

John scooped fresh tobacco into his pipe and tamped it down with his thumb. He struck a match and sucked its flame to the pipe's bowl. The flame shrank and died. He dropped the match into an empty coffee cup and lit another.

Whit wandered to the bookcase. He ran a finger along the rows of books, then pulled out a paperback mystery novel and brought it to his chair.

John frowned at his pipe and set it down. He got up and started toward the kitchen. "Anyway we can have a drink now without corrupting Aaron's innocence," he said. "I could use one. In the attic, Ellie?"

Ellie gathered her thoughts into focus. "On the left side, I think," she said. "Right by that box of photographs."

"Okay." He disappeared around the door and they heard the folding stairs to the attic creak as he pulled them down from the ceiling. His footsteps sounded above them, and something grated over wood. His voice came to them through the air vent, eerily amplified. "There's not much choice," he called. "Bourbon and water be all right with everybody? Whit?"

"Fine," Whit called back. "But a very light one for me, John." He smiled apologetically at Ellie. "You know I don't dare drink much," he explained.

The flimsy stairs rattled under John's feet. There was a clatter of glass and ice from the kitchen, then more footsteps and a final clang as the stairs snapped back into place.

John came in and handed the drinks around. "I got the bottle stashed away," he told them. "But drink fast. That phone might ring any time."

"I hope so," Grace said fervently. She lifted her glass, making it a toast.

Whit's face creased anxiously. "I wonder how long we ought to wait?" he asked.

Grace pursed her lips. "As long as we need to, I should think. We ought to be ready to bring him back, no matter what time he calls."

John twirled his glass between his palms. "Let's give him about another half hour," he said. "That would make it one o'clock. If he hasn't called by then, why don't you two go on home and get some sleep? I'll let you know right away if I hear from him."

"Well, I guess we might as well do that," Whit said. "We won't be any help to poor Aaron if he comes back drunk and we're all too tired to move." He yawned and touched a plump hand to his lips.

Ellie drank in long, slow swallows, feeling the bourbon spread out inside her, warming, loosening a little the knots that held her.

Grace set her glass down. The gentle needle-ticking began again as the woolen square lengthened. On the Christmas tree a blue bulb winked out and then a green one.

Whit lit his pipe. "Poor Aaron," he said. "I know exactly how he must feel now." He nodded several times. Smoke mushroomed out around the pipestem. "Wanting a drink the way he must want one—it's like nothing you can imagine if you haven't gone through it yourself. I used to be sick and shaking. I'd think I couldn't stand it another minute. Poor man."

He flipped the mystery book to the last page and scanned it briefly. Then he slapped the cover shut and put the book on the table. He looked at his watch.

"Well, it's nearly one," he said. "I suppose we might as well all go to bed." He stood up and took his coat from the back of his chair.

Grace folded her knitting and poked it into the fat needlepoint bag that squatted at her feet. She didn't look at her husband. "Whit," she said, "you don't believe he'll come back at all, do you?"

"Any movie in town would have been out a couple of hours ago, dear," Whit said sadly. "No, I'm afraid I don't believe he'll call now. I wish things had turned out differently. But I don't think he'll call."

When Grace looked up tears glinted in her eyes. "I keep thinking about him," she said. "Going off in the night alone that way. And we could have helped him, if he'd let us." She sniffed as she squirmed into the coat Whit held for her.

Ellie uncurled herself from the couch and followed the others to the door. Whit covered her hand with his. "It wasn't your fault, Ellie," he said. "He was just determined to leave, that was all."

He turned to John. "John, you'll let us know." He pulled open the door.

The knot had tightened again in Ellie's throat. "I am so sorry, though," she said to them all.

John put his arm lightly across her shoulders. "Whit's right, Ellie," he said. "There wasn't anything you could have done. Whit, I will call if we hear from him, but it looks as if he's gone."

Ellie watched while Whit and Grace started across the street. Then she closed the door and turned its lock. "You are pretty sure he won't come back now, aren't you?" she asked John.

"About as sure as I can be," he said. "Poor guy."

"Poor Aaron," she agreed.

She started picking the hairpins out of her bun, letting them fall and click onto the glass top of the coffee table. The hair uncoiled and dropped down around her shoulders. It was soft, warming the back of her neck. She shook it free and flipped her fingers through it to loosen the strands. "Poor Aaron," she said again.

"Poor Aaron," John echoed.

Then he laughed. Surprised, she looked up at him. "El, do you know what we sound like?" he asked. "Poor Aaron, poor Aaron—we sound like the Chorus in a Greek tragedy."

He strode forward, then back, his arms folded over his chest. "Poor Aaron," he declaimed ceremoniously.

Then he dropped his arms and laughed again. "Or . . . I just remembered—when I was a kid there was this game we used to play—you bowed to each other and said 'This is a solemn occasion,' very seriously, and you had to keep a straight face."

"Oh! I remember that!" Ellie's smile let loose the taut muscles of her face. "We played that too. It was impossible! You have to look right in each other's eyes all the time and say the words very slowly, and if anybody so much as cracks a smile he's out! I never could do it. I'd always he howling my head off before I'd said two words."

John straightened his mouth to a line, stood off from her, and bowed low. She copied him. They stared at each other, owl-eyed. "This . . . is . . . a . . . solemn . . . occasion," they intoned in unison. They were both laughing as they bowed again.

"Here we go," John announced. " 'Poor Aaron' this time.

84

Now one, two . . ." He swung his arm, conducting. ". . . three!"

Their bows were enormous, sweeping, with hands wide outspread. "Poor . . . Aaron" they mourned together.

Ellie doubled over, laughing, holding her stomach. "I can't stand it!" she gasped.

John took her hand and pulled her up again. "Now," he commanded, and dipped her down once more.

"Poor . . . Aaron. Poor . . . Aaron."

They clung to each other, laughing out of control.

"What's the matter with us?" Ellie gulped. "We're insane."

"Must be the bourbon. It's a shock after the last few days. We're not used to the stuff any more." John rocked back and forth, holding her, wiping his eyes.

"Poor Aaron!" she chanted. "Poor, poor Aaron!"

John grew suddenly quiet. "But really, it is too bad about Aaron," he said.

"Of course it's too bad," she agreed. Then her mouth shook and she was laughing again helplessly. "It's sad," she giggled. "It's so awfully sad, and he's gone gone gone."

"You haven't any charity," John accused her sternly.

"Well, neither have you," she retorted.

He caught her hands and swung her around. "Poor Aaron!" they shouted triumphantly, fitting their voices together. Still holding hands, they ran through the hall and into their bedroom. John kicked the door shut behind them and pushed Ellie to the waiting bed. He dropped down beside her. They held tight to each other, all the laughter ended.

"Poor Aaron," she murmured once more around John's lips.

"Who's Aaron!" he whispered back.

"I don't know," she said.

They struggled out of their clothes, still holding each other, still touching, not wanting to stop touching even that long. They lay on the bedspread naked, skin to skin, pressing close and closer as if they could move into each other through the skin, the firm and well-known naked skin.

The world of people was gone and the children dreaming in their beds were gone and Aaron Sloane was gone totally. Nothing lived but the pair of them, holding, pressing skin to skin down all the length of their two bodies.

His hands moved over her, sparking fire. Then he was on her and she clung to him and the world was fire and bursting light, a hard and silver pounding.

Then the pulsing brightness, like death, like all of life.

Slowly, slowly the brightness subsided. They fell apart from each other, holding gently now, complete. A liquid warmth drowsed in their veins. They pulled the rumpled spread from under them and slid beneath the covers. Body curved to naked body, loosely touching, they slept.

EIGHT

BEFORE THE ALARM CLOCK RANG, ELLIE AWOKE TO SUNLIGHT. THE maple branches framed in the window etched their gold on an ice-blue, polished sky; a sky frozen clean. Sunlight drove into the room through iridescent dust-motes, lay lemony in squares on the bureau, touched to fire the orange spread crumpled at the foot of the bed.

She stretched, lifting her arms high above her head. As she brought them down her hand brushed John's side, warm, naked still. She turned her head to look at him. He lay on his back, his eyes open, hands clasped behind his dark hair. His smile met hers.

She wriggled closer to him, liking the scratchiness of his morning stubble under her cheek, the hardness of his chest bare against her bare breasts.

He pulled her over on top of him and kissed her, squeezing her until she squealed. Then he shoved her back and sat up.

"That's your ration for the morning," he informed her. He grinned. "Tune in tonight for the next thrilling episode."

She giggled and jumped to shut off the alarm as it broke into its raucous jangle.

She hummed as she pulled her robe on, kissed Keith and

Betsy when she met them stumbling sleepy-eyed down the hall. Singing softly, she put on the coffee pot.

"Deck the halls with boughs of holly . . ."

The children squirmed onto their chairs. They were quiet in the way of freshly wakened creatures, hovering still on the edge of dream, uncertain in the daytime world to which they had returned so abruptly.

Keith mashed cornflakes slowly with the back of his spoon. "Mama, do we stay with Grace today?" he wanted to know.

"Yes, you do," Ellie told him cheerfully. "Eat your cereal now, and let's get going."

Betsy looked around the kitchen with blue eyes wide and questioning. "Where Aaron go?" she murmured.

"Aaron isn't here any more, Betsy-o," Ellie said. "He's gone."

Poor Aaron. Where would he be now? She shrugged and poured the coffee. Her happiness this morning would not be weighted down by Aaron. Poor Aaron, of course, but Aaron was gone. Could he really have been so terrible, then, that it was so good to have him gone?

"Come and get it!" she called to John.

Breakfast, dressing—all the ordinary jobs—everything was easy today. Lost shoes found, teeth cleaned . . .

Betsy's hair sprayed out under the brush in a bright, electric-crackling halo. Keith dived behind the Christmas tree for a new puzzle, not to be left behind.

Shoes tied.

"Did you go to the bathroom?"

"Of course you have to take your mittens."

Brief, sideways kisses, wet on Ellie's cheek.

"Quick now, run on over to Grace's. Take Betsy's hand on the street, Keith."

Then she was in the car with John, skimming through the morning, past yards turned from gray to frosted gold, past concrete buildings shining gold. When they pulled up in front of the old Rockfield National Bank she lifted her head to see its poison-green dome glinting back at the sun.

John climbed out of the car and she slid over to the driver's seat. "See you at five, honey," she said. "Have a good day." "You too." He kissed the tip of her nose.

She drove on by herself, singing again. In the parking lot of the library she found a space, pulled into it, and propped the door with her foot while she rummaged through her purse. Lipstick, comb . . .

". . . see the blazing yule before us, fal lal lal . . ."

Pen, kleenex . . .

". . . lal la la . . ."

Lighter, cigarettes . . . The pack was empty. Well, no matter.

But then . . . She pushed her coat sleeve back to uncover her watch. Plenty of time this morning, a few moments longer to be outdoors. She snapped the purse shut and got out of the car. She walked swiftly, half running, to the drugstore at the corner; not to hurry, but because it felt good to move fast in the crisp sunlight. She was humming now, the words singing in her mind. ". . . Strike the harp and join the chorus . . ."

Again, distantly, she wondered, had Aaron been that terrible?

". . . fal la la lal la la . . ." Into the drugstore, faintly chocolate-smelling, fluorescent lighting dimmer than the day.

There was a wide mirror behind the cash register. Waiting there, she could see her face. Cold air and running had pulled the blood in under the skin of her cheeks. Her wide apart gray-green eyes were alive. Even the hair straggling from her scarf was alive with a brightness that made it seem gold as much as brown. Was she twenty-eight? Yesterday, Christmas, she had been old, so old. But this morning . . .

The yawning clerk was holding out her change. She took it from him and gave him such a smile that his yawn changed half through and he smiled in answer.

As she turned from the counter an imperative voice sounded behind her. "Ellie Clark!"

She swung around to meet a determined narrow face between slabs of short-clipped rusty hair. Wilma Kirkland. Beside Wilma stood a young, square-jawed man with a light grin and a heavy blond wave.

"Ellie, you're a stranger," Wilma accused. She turned to the man. "Ellie lives right down the street, Byron, and we never see her. Never see her at all. Well, she's busy, I suppose, and of course we're all busy, aren't we? But Ellie, you must come to see us."

"I will," Ellie promised.

Wilma stepped nearer, and her coat swung about her angular body as loosely as if it were on a hanger. "Ellie, you must meet Byron." A jerk of the narrow head indicated the blond man. "Byron Richardson, you know—I must have told you he was coming to visit, I've been telling everybody. My big sister's boy. From Chicago. I mean Byron lives in Chicago now—Jeanne Louise is still back in Pittsburgh, of course."

She gave a single laugh, and looked to her nephew to share the small joke.

"Byron is just out of dental school, Ellie. He's in practice in Chicago—has an office with two other dentists there, older men, very successful, I understand, both of them—that's such a good way for a young man to get started, I always think."

Her smile pulled her lips back from over-large front teeth. "Ellie, I can't tell you how wonderful it's been having Byron here for the holidays. George, Junior can't ever get back, it seems—I really don't think Edna likes to travel with the babies, and California is so far away. But I'm afraid Byron hasn't had enough to keep him busy while he's been with us.

Rockfield must be pretty dull after Chicago. Isn't it, Byron?

She looked at him knowingly. His forehead grew a little redder under the brush of hair.

Can a woman leer, Ellie wondered. Wilma could.

"Of course there is our New Year's party Saturday," Wilma went on. "Byron will still be here for that, and you'll be coming too, Ellie. So that will be nice."

She's commanding it to be nice, Ellie thought. How would it dare be otherwise?

Byron met Ellie's eyes with a grin. He tilted his head toward his aunt and shrugged.

Wilma was looking at her watch. "My word," she said, "it's later than I thought. We'll have to go along now, Ellie, we have some things to do this morning."

"Wilma's so scared I'll get bored she hasn't given me time to think," Byron said. His voice went with his face. It was a nice voice, an easy bass. "But up till now she's been hiding all the girls from me." His eyes were easy too, the look in them appreciative, interested. A man-and-woman look.

"I'll be seeing you, Byron," Ellie said. "Goodbye, Wilma."

Wilma was halfway to the door. "Saturday!" she reminded. "Any time after nine."

Ellie felt happier than ever as she watched them leave the drugstore. Light, almost giddy. Unreasonably, it delighted her that Wilma hadn't mentioned John or the children, had called her only "Ellie Clark." It delighted her for no deeper reason than that it was so good to see that look in a man's eyes and know it was for her, that she could still bring it out.

But by the time she was stepping briskly through the sunshine again, her thoughts had leapt to John, to the way it had been last night, to the way it would be this night. Wilma Kirkland's nephew was all but forgotten.

She ran up the wide steps of the library, swished through the glass doors, heels clicking gaily on marble. She ran the marble stairs from bottom to top, gave the clock a pat, then slowed with an effort to cross the reading room.

Maybe she would feed the children early. Then after they were in bed, she and John would have dinner alone. With candles in the tall wooden candlesticks, and wine.

"Hi, Whit, you here?" she called as she came into the office.

Steak? Yes, definitely steak. A good one. She'd buy it on the way home.

"Good morning, Ellie." The tiredness in Whit's voice surprised her. Everyone should be as happy today as she was. But Whit had wanted to help Aaron.

She pulled the cover from her typewriter and sat down. She was typing fast, liking the swift, even ticking of the keys, the certainty of her flying fingers, when the associate librarian appeared in the doorway.

Miss Headen stood straight in her severe blue blouse and black skirt. (Was there only one skirt and blouse, worn daily, Ellie wondered suddenly. Or was there an identical wardrobe of them?) Miss Headen's sharp face was pasted around by waves of yellowed white hair, as stiff as if it had been cut from cardboard. She looked at Ellie through rimless glasses as she might look at a spot on the spotless skirt. "I would like to speak with Mr. Meade," she said.

"Whit!" Ellie called. The typewriter keys jammed. Why was she always flustered around this woman?

Miss Headen looked more disapproving than ever.

Whit came around the partition. He seemed worried. Deep lines climbed the slope of his forehead. He was rubbing the corners of his eyes. "Yes, Alma?" he asked, tiredly, pleasantly.

"Mr. Meade," Miss Headen said, "there was someone to see you." She paused, interlocking narrow fingers in front of her skirt band.

"You may send him on in, Alma," Whit said.

"It was a woman. She has left now." Miss Headen stood still in the doorway, not moving, as if she were waiting for something. Ellie wondered what the matter was.

"Well, did the woman say what she wanted?" A controlled impatience had crept into Whit's thin voice.

"I asked her to leave," Miss Headen explained severely. "She seemed to be . . . I am convinced that she is . . . well." She bit the sentence to an end. Whit frowned.

"Mr. Meade, she began asking for you as soon as she came into the library. She asked everyone she met. She knew your name. I took her message—she had a note for you. Here it is." She pulled a folded piece of paper from her skirt pocket and laid it on Ellie's desk, letting her fingertips rest on it as if she hated to give it up.

"I decided it would be better if she didn't see you herself, Mr. Meade. You know Mr. Stone is here—he comes in most mornings to see the *Times*. There are a number of others in the reading room too. They were all noticing the woman, I thought, and it didn't seem wise . . ."

Again she bit the sentence off.

"You know Mr. Stone is on the Library Board," she began again. "And it was really quite obvious what the woman was. She did know your name, you see, Mr. Meade."

Ellie thought she saw something that was nearly a smile brush over Miss Headen's colorless lips.

"The woman told me she was walking by the jail a short while ago when a man called to her from a window and asked her to wait." Miss Headen's voice lifted with her eyebrows when she said the word "jail." "It seems that the man was someone she . . . knew. He threw this note down to her from the jail window. He told her he needed help badly, and asked her to bring the note here, to you. He told her you would understand." Again the eyebrows questioned.

93

"I am certain Mr. Stone was listening to her, Mr. Meade, her voice was rather loud."

Ellie's throat tightened, as if with an old pain. Jail. Aaron? Of course, Aaron.

Whit smoothed his fringe of hair and cleared his throat. "All right, Alma," he said. "Thank you." He reached for the paper. It looked like a sheet torn from a school tablet. He shook it open and held it on the desk with a finger while he hooked his glasses awkwardly over his ears. "Thank you, Alma," he said again, determinedly. "I'll take care of this."

Miss Headen's mouth stretched thinner as she turned and marched back to the reading room.

Whit bent over Ellie's desk, leaning his elbows on it, moving his lips silently. Ellie stretched to see. On the paper the words were pencilled in a small, neatly curved script:

> Mr. Meade, I am in jail again. I am sorry. I was drunk. Mr. Meade, I know how much trouble I've been to you people. You shouldn't have tried to help me. I'm not worth it. I won't ask you for any more help, but would you mind if I just stay out in your car nights till I can get in the alcoholic place? I get out of here later today. I know now I can't stand jail any more, I have to get fixed up. I won't bother you. I won't even come in your house.
>
> Aaron Avery Sloane

Whit straightened and put the glasses back in his pocket. He walked slowly to the window and rested his head against the frame. "Oh dear," was all he said.

"Whit?" Ellie asked. She held her voice steady. "Whit are you going to let him stay?"

Whit didn't lift his head. "Of course I can't make him sleep in the car," he murmured, so low he might have been talking to himself. He tapped a rhythm on the window pane.

94

Then he turned to her. "He's been drinking the way he does for twenty years," he said. "Twenty years—that's a long time. I don't think he'll be able to stop without a lot of help. A lot of patience. We're the only ones around to help him. If we give him up now . . ."

He walked back to the desk and picked up the note. He stood a moment, holding it, frowning at it. "Maybe we're the last chance Aaron will ever have," he said.

He folded the paper carefully, sharpening the creases between a thumb and forefinger. He looked off from Ellie, away through the window.

"I felt the way Aaron feels, once," he said. "I was never terribly drunk, never so drunk I couldn't do what I had to do. But I was never really sober, either, from the time I got up in the morning until I went to bed at night. I was afraid to be completely sober. I could have finished up just like Aaron. But a few people were patient with me then."

His eyes came back to Ellie. "I didn't deserve any help," he said, "but they helped me. It was all the difference in the world for me."

He slid the note into his pocket. "Yes, I'll ask him to stay with us again," he said. "I think I'll go on to the jail and see him now. For me it only means another few days."

He started toward the coat rack, then turned. "By the way, Ellie, John doesn't have to be in on this if he doesn't want to be."

"If I know John, he'll want to help," Ellie said.

She ran a finger across the top row of typewriter keys, listening to the series of tiny ticks. What's he like now, she wondered. The way he was last night? Or different, now he's been in jail again?

She shivered. She felt weighted to the floor with an old heaviness like a block of stone.

95

Whit was fumbling at the coat rack, bringing down his overcoat. "I'm not sure just how long I'll be gone, Ellie," he said. "Alma can take care of things. I might stay at the jail for a while and just talk to him. I've an idea that's what he needs as much as he needs a place to stay."

NINE

HEAVILY AND SLOWLY THE DAY HAD GONE TO EVENING. ELLIE perched on a stool by Grace's sink, staring at the group around the kitchen table. Her eyes were half-focused, refused to focus. The hazy figures across the room looked almost posed.

Aaron Sloane, released, was at one end of the table. He had on a clean shirt—Whit's? His pants were freshly pressed. He crouched over a narrow strip of leather, stippling it with a large nail held firmly in one strong hand. His cigarette jumped on his lip each time the nail hit the leather.

Whit and John, each braced on an elbow, watched him closely from either side. Grace hovered behind them all, pink-faced and glowing, cradling a towel-wrapped coffee pot.

Suddenly Ellie thought of da Vinci's *Last Supper*. Aaron and his apostles. She blinked her eyes to clear them. What do you want, Ellie Clark—a world all to yourself?

In spite of her the figures blurred again. Once Aaron Sloane was the outsider. Now they're all together, she thought, all of them. Whit and Grace. John. Revolving around their alcoholic like planets around the sun. I can't join them. All I can do its pretend. I'm the one outside.

She sat apart, alone, wrapped in space. Looking on. And

97

saw, irrelevantly, the eyes of the young dentist—what was his name? Wilma's nephew, in the drugstore, when she had been so happy. Just this morning. She saw the attentive look his eyes had held for her.

She shook her head, shaking away those eyes. Aaron needs help. Aaron is sick. Aaron is desperate.

It sounded like a litany. Damn.

The tapping had stopped. Aaron was squinting critically at the leather strip. The leather had been Grace's idea, to give him something to do. He had done leather work in prison, he'd told her.

"This piece is sort of stiff, isn't it, Miz Meade?" he said. "You had it a long time?"

Grace peered over his shoulder. "Oh, I guess it must have been in the attic four or five years," she said. "It's left from some I bought for Whit once, one time when Whit was feeling a little bit depressed. I thought it would help him if he could do something with his hands—you know? There used to be some real leather tools, but I think we finally gave them away."

"I never was much good with leather," Whit explained apologetically. "I just don't have the patience for it or something."

"Takes a lot of patience," Aaron agreed. He took up the nail and dug the side of its point into the resisting surface.

"Whit did make me a beautiful key-case," Grace said. "And he started on a belt for himself, Aaron. But he never finished the belt. He got pretty busy about that time—some extra things came up at the library, I believe—and anyway he was feeling better by then."

"Was it really only four beers you had last night, Aaron?" John asked abruptly.

Aaron glanced at him. "Well, these cops know me, Mr. Clark," he said. "I don't have to drink much. If they see me around town when I've had anything at all they just pick me right up."

He bent to the leather again. His hardened thumb worked in the nail. "It's the same in any town where I've been in jail."

"Why, I think that's terrible!" Grace declared. "It's . . . it's judging a man guilty until he can be proved innocent. Instead of the other way around."

She reached around Aaron with the coffee pot. As she bent over him, filling his cup, her heavy breast brushed his shoulder.

Ellie stared. Had that been on purpose? No, surely not. Her own breast felt a stab of cold.

Whit's forehead reddened. He set his own cup down and Ellie saw coffee slosh into his saucer.

John was busy with his pipe, scraping out the bowl with a tiny knife, tamping in the fresh tobacco. "Well, with this arrest on the record it'll be another seventy-two hours before they'll take you at the alcoholic center," he said. "Seventy-two hours from, say, ten or eleven last night. Would that be about right?" He lit a match and sucked the flame into the pipe in little kissing spurts.

Grace set the coffee pot back on the stove. Then she pulled a chair close to Aaron and sat down. She put a hand on his sleeve. Her eyes were soft with concern. "How do you feel now, Aaron?" she asked him gently. "Is there anything I can do for you?"

Aaron laid down the nail. He turned to Grace and seemed to study her. His eyes narrowed to slits. Slowly, not moving his eyes from her, he pulled another cigarette from the pack in his shirt pocket and pushed it into the side of his mouth. He took out a match folder, tore off the last match, struck it, and held it to the cigarette. Still watching her, he crumpled the empty folder and dropped it on the table. He blew out a line of smoke.

99

Then he grunted and turned back to the bit of leather, pressing the nail in steadily.

Ellie shivered, wondering.

John's pipe glowed up and faded. "That would make it late Wednesday night," he said thoughtfully. "Only I suppose the admissions wouldn't be open until Thursday morning. Perhaps we could run him over to Cedarville early, Whit, before work, do you think?

Whit was rubbing his small eyes as if they hurt him. "Thursday morning," he said. "Yes. Yes, certainly. First thing Thursday morning."

"I've been reading about this alcoholic center, Aaron," John said. "They have a good program. There's occupational therapy, all sorts of group activities . . ."

Aaron's head jerked up. "They don't lock you in, do they?" he demanded. "That lady social worker—the one that talked to me in prison—she said they wouldn't lock me in."

"Oh no," John said. "It's open. It's not a prison, Aaron. It's just a kind of hospital, for people who want to stop drinking."

"I don't want to be locked up," Aaron said. He tugged the cigarette from his mouth. "That lady said there were two alcoholic places in Cedarville. The other one's part of the nut-house there. It's a lock-up. I can't stand it in a lock-up."

"Of course you wouldn't want to be locked in, Aaron," Grace cried. "That would be terrible for you. After just getting out of jail."

Aaron scraped back his chair. He paced to the black window behind the table. He smacked the glass with the flat of his hand. He turned back to them. "Sometimes, in jail . . . I've spent whole nights at the door, sometimes, up against the bars. There were some places I couldn't have stood it if they hadn't had such a wide door."

The cigarette trembled in his fingers. "You can't put me in any lock-up."

John went to him, touched his shoulder. "Aaron, I can promise they won't lock you up at the alcoholic center," he said.

Whit cleared his throat. "Any coffee left, dear?" he asked Grace.

"I think so," she said. She brought the pot and filled his cup absently, her eyes following Aaron as he shuffled restlessly back and forth.

Whit got up, a little stiffly. He carried his coffee to where Ellie sat, by the sink. He slumped against the counter beside her. "The children seem to be sleeping well," he remarked.

Ellie turned to him, embarrassed. "Oh, yes," she said. "They're so used to being over here. They drop right off."

"Yes," he said. He cleared his throat again and stirred the coffee, staring morosely into the cup. She could think of nothing else to say to him.

Grace . . . Aaron . . . What had been decided that moment at the table? Or had there been any moment?

John was looking at the strip of leather. "Let's see what you've got here, Aaron," he said. "Why, this is good!"

Aaron came back. "Yes, I got to be pretty good with leather," he said, "I've made a lot of things in prison. The other men—they usually get me to make things for them."

John brought the strip to Whit and Ellie. On the dampened surface the name AARON AVERY SLOANE had appeared as if magically, raised in slanted letters against a grainy background. At each end of the name was an intricate small shape—a swirled blossom, perhaps, or a leaf.

"It's nice," Ellie murmured.

Grace came and took it in her hands. "Why Aaron, it's perfectly beautiful!" she exclaimed. "Whit worked and worked at designs with those expensive tools I bought him, but they still weren't as good as this. And you did it all with that old nail!"

"You seem to be very talented, Aaron," said Whit. His high forehead flushed and faded.

Aaron's mouth twitched at a corner. "I never did use those regular tools," he said. "They're not heavy enough. You have to hammer on them. In prison I used to fix me up a tool out of a nail setting punch. I'd flatten down the point of it. There was always some kind of workshop where I could fix it. I could do a real good job with a punch like that."

"Nail setting punch," Whit said dully. "Yes."

"Would you let me have it, Miz Meade?" Aaron asked. "Just a couple of spots I want to smooth out here."

He took the strip from Grace and sat down. He bent over the leather, grinding in the nail, rounding, evening, deepening. After a moment he straightened and rubbed his eyes.

"Kind of hard to see this close work," he said. "I had some glasses—just for reading and work like this—but I lost them somewhere. When I was arrested, maybe, that other time."

"Whit," Grace asked, "could Aaron see through your glasses, do you think? They're just reading glasses, too, Aaron. Magnifying glasses."

"Oh no, Miz Meade," Aaron protested. "I wouldn't want to take your husband's glasses."

Grace's soft lips smiled confidently. "It's all right, Aaron," she assured him. "Whit wouldn't mind. Would you, dear?"

Whit's mouth tightened. He pulled his glasses from his pocket without a word and took them to Aaron. Then he sat down and rubbed his hands over his round face. Uncomfortably, Ellie watched him.

Aaron fitted the glasses on and blinked. His pale eyes looked unfamiliar behind the lenses. "They'll do fine," he said. "Thank you, Mr. Meade."

He went to work again with his nail. He dotted the leather

swiftly, mechanically, like a woodpecker tapping insects from a tree. He paused and dug again. Then more woodpecker tapping.

At last he laid the nail on the table and leaned back. Pleased little half-moon lines creased his sunken cheeks. His fear seemed vanished. He smoothed his hair down and looked at John.

"You know what I'd like to do, Mr. Clark?" he asked. "I'd like to make something for you people. You've all done so much for me, when you didn't have to. I'd like to make you a present to show you I appreciate it. I couldn't buy the leather now, of course. But someday I will. Someday when I can I'll make you something and send it to you. Maybe . . ."

He blinked upward through Whit's glasses. "Maybe a couple of pocketbooks for Miz Meade and Miz Clark—I can make good pocketbooks. Real good ones, that'll last a long time. I mean to do that for you when I can."

"Oh Aaron!" Grace exclaimed. "You can't know how much it would mean to me to have a pocketbook you'd made. Aaron, you could work on them now, while you're here with us. It might pass the time. Would you do it if we bought you the leather and all?"

She took her husband's arm. "We could get the things for him, couldn't we, Whit?"

John looked at Whit thoughtfully. "That does sound like a good idea," he said. "I'd share the cost, of course."

Aaron's mouth twitched. "I'd be pleased to do that," he told them all.

Grace was rummaging through a drawer by the sink. She pulled out a torn envelope and a pencil and laid them in front of Aaron. "Just put down everything you'll need, Aaron," she said. "Whit and John can pick it up for you."

Aaron tapped his chin with the pencil. "Well, let me think

what it would take," he said. "There would be the leather, suede for liners, buckles, leather varnish . . ."

Shaking his head, he put the pencil down. "No. No, I couldn't let you pay for all that. Be ten or fifteen dollars for good materials. I'd want the ladies to have good pocketbooks, that would last. No, I'll wait till I'm out of that hospital, till I have some money of my own." He pushed the envelope away from him.

John leaned forward. "Please let us buy the things for you, Aaron," he said. "Your work is what will make them special."

"Oh yes, Aaron," Grace agreed. "Don't worry about the money one bit."

"We can take care of it," Whit said without looking at Aaron.

John's eyes caught Ellie's, calling her to say something, be something. Be one of them. "I would like a pocketbook very much, Aaron," she said.

Her voice was wrong, too formal. Half-memories . . . Thank you for the lovely doll, Aunt Lucy . . . and do I have to take Aunt Lucy with the doll? Does Aaron Sloane go with the pocketbook? And what can I say?

"Then it's all settled," Grace stated. "Now just write down what you'll need, Aaron." She put the pencil in his hand as if he were a child.

"If you're sure you want me to," he said. The thin lips twitched up again. Swiftly he wrote a few lines and handed the envelope to John. "There, I think that's everything. I saw a leather store downtown, Mr. Clark. Near Mr. Guffy's place, I think it was."

John nodded. "I'll find it," he said. "I'll try to get out on my lunch hour tomorrow."

As he stuffed the envelope into his pocket his throat filled out with a hidden yawn. "Getting late," he said. "Ellie, you can get Betsy and I'll bring Keith. We won't even have to wake them up."

Released, Ellie went to the living room. The children were asleep on the long couch; Betsy curled mouse-like into a ball. Keith sprawled on his back with an arm and a leg flung over the side. Ellie put on her own coat and then gathered up Betsy in the blanket that covered her; carried her snugly wrapped, back to the kitchen.

John had Aaron's piece of leather again, admiring it. Ellie didn't go to him. She wanted shadow, wanted to be unnoticed. Someone had left a chair near the back door, in a dim corner formed by Grace's tall freezer. She sat there now, not wanting to have to talk to anyone, not wanting to have to pretend. She was the outsider.

John put the leather down and went for Keith. Whit followed him. Ellie, rubbing her cheek idly over Betsy's smooth hair, could hear them talking in the next room. Or John talking, rather; low, earnest. Planning, arranging, taking a man's life under protection.

She was the outsider. But it's not safe, outside. John had always kept her safe.

She sat alone in the dimness, unnoticed, half hidden by the freezer's bulk. Outside.

Grace moved between table and sink, stacking the cups and saucers, scraping, rinsing. Aaron stayed, watching her, smoking steadily. Once he glanced toward the corner where Ellie was and saw her waiting there. He stared at her for a moment with a look she didn't understand. A considering look. Then his eyes went neutral.

He stubbed his cigarette out. He stood up, ignoring Ellie, and walked slowly over to Grace. "Miz Meade, would you mind if I said something to you?" he asked. His voice was level.

Quickly Grace turned off the faucet. "What is it, Aaron?" Her cheeks grew pinker.

"Well," Aaron said, "I just wanted to tell you something, Miz Meade. It's about some people I was staying with one time, doing some work for them. They were nice people to stay with. Real nice people. That was what I thought at first, anyway. The wife was good to me, just like you are, Miz Meade. And she was pretty, too."

He looked at Grace's bright lips, a little parted now. His eyes crept down to her generous bosom, her resolutely flattened stomach.

"That woman did a lot for me," he said. "Cooked real good food for me, even bought me new clothes. Just because she liked me and felt sorry for me, she said. Then one day when her husband wasn't home she got me in the bedroom." He smiled, a quick small smile.

Grace gripped the edge of the sink. "Oh," she said.

Ellie bit at her lip. She shifted Betsy higher on her lap, wanting to pick her up and leave, not knowing how to leave.

"I guess she did like me," Aaron went on. "And she was some woman. Some woman." The light eyes stared directly into Grace's. Grace looked down.

"Well, what happened," Aaron said, "was that her husband came home about that time. He came in calling his wife, and what did he do but find us there in the bedroom."

Grace's eyes, wide open, flew again to his. He met them.

"That man was so mad at me I didn't know for a while if I'd get out of it alive," he said. "He wasn't any bigger than me, but when he pushed through that bedroom door he looked like a truck coming down on me. He wasn't mad at his wife at all, and it was her that had started it. He was just mad at me. But it was like he didn't know what to do either. He just stood there looking at me like he'd kill me next, and I got out of there fast."

106

Grace pressed her fingers to her mouth.

"He called the police then and had me arrested before I had time to get out of town," Aaron said.

"What happened?" Grace whispered.

"Well, they put me in jail. The husband said I'd raped his wife, and that woman went along with every word he said." Aaron shook his head unbelievingly. "That woman that looked so nice. She told everybody I'd raped her."

He reached in his shirt pocket for another cigarette and held it loosely in his palm. Grace stared at him wordlessly, her hand still to her mouth.

"There was going to be a trial," he said. "But then some lawyer came to see me and he told the two of them they'd better not press charges. Said if there was a trial it would just be what I said about it against what they said about it. Said the jury might feel sorry for me and let me off." He put the cigarette btween his lips and struck a match.

"Maybe that lawyer felt sorry for me too." He bent to light the cigarette. "I was pretty scared, I don't mind saying."

He tossed the match past Grace into the sink. "Yes, Miz Meade, I was scared all right. I've been in prison right much, but not for rape."

Grace's eyes swam with tears. She reached out a hand to touch his arm. "Oh Aaron," she said. "What a terrible woman. They could have put you in prison for the rest of your life! Or . . . who knows what."

Her fingers pressed his arm more tightly. "Oh Aaron," she said again, softly. "I wish I could make up for everything that's ever happened to you! I wish I could make it all as if it had never happened."

Ellie shrank deeper into the shadow. She was cold. She had to get out somehow. What could she say?

Aaron pulled away from Grace and looked at her steadily. "Miz Meade," he said, "when they let me out of jail that time

I made up my mind I'd never get mixed up with a woman when I was staying in the house with her and her husband." He moved a step back. "I don't want to take any chances, Miz Meade. I'd rather die than spend my whole life in jail." He strode to the table. "I'd rather die." He smashed his cigarette into an ashtray and lit another. He came back to Grace. "I can have a woman any time I want one, Miz Meade," he said. A thin stream of smoke breathed from his nostrils. "Any time. Never any trouble. They like me." His mouth twitched.

"Some I pay, when I've been working. Some I don't pay. They like me."

He looked again into Grace's eyes. "But I'm not going to get mixed up with any woman when I'm staying in the house with her and her husband. I just wanted to tell you."

Grace squeezed the collar of her dress. Her knuckles were white. "Oh Aaron!" she said. "I'm not . . . I wouldn't . . ."

She stopped and looked at him with widened eyes. Then she looked down, out, away from him. For the first time she saw Ellie, motionless in the corner, clutching Betsy. She reddened and jerked her hand down from her collar, lifted it again to poke her hair into place. She threw the sink faucet on as hard as it would go.

"I just wanted to tell you, Miz Meade," Aaron said evenly. "I want you to know you're perfectly safe with me. Now I think I'll go to bed."

TEN

THE TELEPHONE PURRED POLITELY THROUGH THE EVEN TICKING
of typewriter keys. Without moving her eyes from her paper
Ellie lifted the receiver and cradled it between her cheek and
upraised shoulder. "Rockfield Public Library. Good morning."

"Ellie." Grace's voice was sharp. "I've got to talk to Whit.
Ellie, that man is just impossible. Whit and John will have
to do something about him. It's getting beyond all reason."

Ellie's hand jumped to hold the receiver more surely.
"Aaron? Grace, what's wrong? Are Keith and Betsy . . ."

"Does nothing but beg for a drink," Grace interrupted.
"Constantly. Won't leave me in peace for a minute. I found
him just now going through the things in the medicine cabinet—looking for cough medicine, I suppose, or anything that
might have alcohol in it. I tell him we don't have anything to
drink—I tell him he musn't have anything, and he goes away
and then he's right back the next minute begging again. He
looks wild, too. I can't handle him, Ellie. I just give up."

"Grace, are the children all right?" Ellie got out.

"Children?" Grace sounded baffled. "Yes, they're all right.
Oh, Betsy was crying a while ago, but I . . . oh, Ellie, just do

buzz Whit for me. He has to do something about that wild man!"

"All right," Ellie said. She jabbed a button at the base of the telephone and listened until she heard the click of Whit's receiver.

Grace was bitter. Ellie had never heard her bitter about anyone before. Then had Aaron's story last night meant what it seemed to mean—and had he been right about Grace?

Ellie leaned to look out the door, at the big clock. Eleven-twenty-three. Not long before noon.

Wild. Worse than he was Christmas night?

Betsy cries a lot—Grace wasn't worried about her. All three-year-olds cry.

She made herself touch the typewriter again, made herself transfer meaningless words to the paper in it, tried to type the clock hands along.

He wants a drink, she told herself. Just a drink. It hasn't anything to do with the children.

Why couldn't I ask why Betsy was crying? Anybody else would ask.

Again she leaned to see the clock. Eleven thirty-two. She chewed the side of her thumb. Calm down, Ellie Clark. Don't you believe he's safe, by now? Grace can take care of those children.

Eleven thirty-six.

Grace can't handle him.

It's nothing to do with the children.

Why was Betsy crying? Damn.

She ripped a bit of paper from the tablet on her desk and scribbled a note for Whit. Then she snatched her coat from the rack and ran out of the office, tying on her scarf as she ran.

She didn't know what she expected to find when she came

into the Meade's kitchen. Panic . . . broken furniture . . . a television scene of chaos . . .

But there was Grace at the sink counter, with lips compressed, rolling dough to a thin sheet. Keith and Betsy stood on chairs beside her, swathed in towels, pressing out flowers and trees and four-leafed clovers with cookie cutters. Betsy's flour-spattered face opened in a brilliant smile when she saw her mother. Keith looked at her briefly without interest, and went back to his cutting.

"Hello, Ellie," Grace said. There was a tight-drawn look about Grace's eyes. She pushed the back of her hand across her forehead, leaving a streak of white. "Aaron's in the living room. Maybe you could say something to him. Heaven knows I've tried." She banged the rolling pin mercilessly onto the dough.

"Well . . ." Ellie glanced toward the living room door. "Grace, what was the matter with the children? When you called?"

"The children?" Grace looked blank.

"Betsy. You said she was crying. Did . . . what was wrong?"

"Crying? She wasn't—oh, I guess she did cry some, earlier. It was something or other about a toy. Keith had it and she wanted it, or I don't know what. It's all right now. I just gave them each a cookie and they forgot about it. Ellie, please do go and talk to him. He'll be raging in here for a drink again any minute. I wish I never had to lay eyes on him again."

Grace bent over the counter, picking flecks of dough from the rolling pin with a fingernail. She looked quickly up at Ellie, then looked away from her. "I guess you heard what he was saying to me last night. I still can't figure out what he meant by all that."

"Well, I guess I could tell him hello," Ellie said uncomfortably.

She went to the living room. Aaron was striding back and forth, not slowing even when he turned. A cigarette wobbled in the corner of his mouth. He looked worse than Ellie had ever seen him, worse even than he had looked Christmas night. His legs seemed to crumple each time a foot met the floor. His cheeks and chin were gray with stubble, and his hair bristled in every direction. Around his eyes the skin puffed and sagged. His shirt was wrinkled. She had never seen him in a wrinkled shirt before.

Grace's wine-red carpet was littered with cigarette butts.

"How are you, Aaron?" she asked timidly. There must be other, better questions to ask.

He stopped in the middle of the floor. "Not good, Miz Clark," he said. "Not good. I don't know if I can make it." He threw his cigarette down and ground it into the carpet's pile, another smudge of gray in the wine-red.

"If I could have a drink, just one drink, even, maybe I could make it."

"Oh, you'll be all right, Aaron," Ellie said helplessly. "It's not very long to wait. I know you'll be all right."

Not very long. But it's too long, she thought, too long for all of us. She ran back to the kitchen before he could say anything more.

Grace had set cups on the table and was splashing coffee into them. "Well, you saw how he is," she said.

Ellie nodded. She watched Grace bang around the kitchen, shoving cookies onto a platter, slamming it down on the table. Grace with lips pressed firmly, a disapproving frown creased between her neatly traced eyebrows. All the sympathy, all the warmth, were gone.

The kitchen was too quiet. "Grace, where did the children go?" Ellie asked.

"They're making a hop-scotch in the basement. I sent them down there with chalk and a dish of cookies."

Grace nudged the cat from the chair where it had been sleeping. It stretched and arched and swayed away from her. "Whit said he'd try to come home if he could. I think he's calling around to get some professional advice about Aaron. We need some."

She went to the living room door. "Aaron," she called. "Coffee, if you want it." Her voice was dry. It would have held more welcome if she had been calling a dog for scraps.

Aaron appeared like a specter in the doorway. "I don't want coffee, Miz Meade," he said. "I just want a drink. Not much. If you could give me anything."

He shuffled to the table and held the edge of it, not looking at either of them. "Please, Miz Meade. I'm sick. You don't know how it is. I just can't take it."

Grace's scowl etched into her forehead. "No, Aaron," she said. "No, and that's all. Now here is the coffee. And cookies."

"Please, Miz Meade," he said.

A spasm of coughing shook him. His hand knocked against the cup. It clattered to its side. Coffee poured in a black river across the tablecloth. He stumbled out of the kitchen and they could hear him, still coughing harshly, bang shut his bedroom door.

Grace reached for a towel. "Those men are going to have to do something," she said. "I can't. I'm fed up."

Ellie drank her coffee, watching Grace's closed and angry face.

She was glad when the back door opened and Whit and John came in. A burst of cold air came with them, cutting like sudden sanity through the kitchen's heat. There was a purposefulness in John's jaw that Ellie had not seen there for days. Whit's round face looked almost cheerful.

"We've been making some phone calls," John said. "It seems that Aaron can get into the regular state mental hospital right away. They do take alcoholics. It's not quite as good as the rehabilitation center, but for Aaron it could be what he needs. There's no waiting period. He can go any time, drunk or sober. Whit and I thought we'd take time off from work and drive him over there right now."

He took a pink frosted reindeer from the cookie platter and popped it whole into his mouth.

"The mental hospital?" Ellie asked. "Isn't that the 'lock-up' Aaron's so afraid of?"

"Well, yes, I suppose it is," John said. "But it seems to be the only place for him now. He can't stay dry for any three days. We've seen that."

Whit poured himself a cup of coffee. "We thought Aaron was a candidate for the rehabilitation center," he said. "But he's been an alcoholic for so long. Twenty years or more. He's afraid of any hospital. Going without a drink for seventy-two hours, scared to death all the time—that's too much to expect of him. Almost inhuman."

He dropped a spoonful of sugar into his cup. His voice broke and went higher like an adolescent's. "Much better to put him in the mental hospital, where they can take care of him now. Besides, the people we talked to weren't sure he could profit from the rehabilitation center, even assuming he could get in. They thought he was probably too far gone."

"The admissions at the mental hospital are for thirty-day periods," John said. "Aaron's been locked up in jail for enough thirty day stretches. One more in a good hospital won't kill him."

"That's the first sense we've heard lately," Grace declared. "He's back in his room if you want to go get him."

"Come on, Whit," John said. "Let's talk to him." Ellie watched their two backs move militantly out of the kitchen.

Grace brushed a loop of hair back from her forehead. "Well thank goodness," she said. "It's high time somebody

114

put Aaron where he could be taken care of. The lock-up is welcome to him."

Her eyes darted around the kitchen. "I think I'll fix them some sandwiches to take along," she said. "They'll want lunch."

Ellie leaned back and lit a cigarette. The menthol was cool in her throat. Breathing it in, she listened to the voices from the spare bedroom. Just sounds, the words lost among walls and rugs. John's voice, firm and resonant; Whit's, high, scraping, just as determined. An occasional rumble from Aaron.

Aaron would really be gone. Soon now.

Then John and Whit were back, with Aaron behind them. Aaron sank to a chair and pressed the palms of his hands over his closed eyes.

John's cheeks looked gray, the line between his eyebrows deep. The firmness had left his mouth. Whit's face was bleak.

Whit cleared his throat. "Aaron feels pretty badly about the hospital idea," he said.

Aaron moved his head slowly from side to side, not lifting it from his hands. "I can't stand any lock-up, Mr. Meade, he said. His words were steady, uninflected, so low they could hardly hear them. "I've been in too many lock-ups. I can't stand it. Too many lock-ups."

His hands dropped to the table. He stared straight in front of him, seeing what none of them could see. "I was in solitary confinement. You don't know what it's all about till you've been in solitary." His eyes wrinkled shut as if with pain. "It's the worst thing there is. I can't stand any more."

Ellie's stomach clenched. She looked anxiously at the faces around her. Whit's, worried. Grace's, sullen, lips pressed together. John's.

John spoke gently. "The hospital wouldn't be like solitary,

Aaron," he said. "They do have to lock the doors, but it's not a prison. You could get well there."

"You could get well and never have to be in a prison again," Whit put in, talking quickly.

Aaron buried his face again. His shoulders trembled. "I can't stand it," he said. "I can't stand a lock-up. And all those crazy people. Don't make me go there. I don't know what I'd do if you made me go there. I'd kill myself."

John leaned back against the wall. "We can't force you to go, Aaron," he said. "We won't have you committed. All we're asking is for you to let us take you there so you can admit yourself. It's just for a month."

He went to the table and touched Aaron's shoulder. "Aaron, it's nothing like a month of jail. Can't you understand that this is the only way to help yourself?"

Aaron brought his head up slowly. He looked straight at John. "Don't take me to that lock-up, Mr. Clark," he said. "I want you to promise not to make me go there." His words were spaced. His voice was commanding, as it had been to Ellie Christmas night. A level voice, not to be disobeyed.

John paced to the sink. He shoved his fists in his pockets and turned to Aaron. "All right," he said at last. "We won't take you there."

"I can't stand any lock-up," Aaron said once more, looking still into John's eyes. "Not any kind of lock-up." He walked out of the kitchen.

Whit watched him go. "So we'll have to keep him," he said. He sat in the chair Aaron had left and stared through the window to the pattern of bare branches beyond it.

Grace sat beside him and put her hand on his. "Honey," she asked him, "is there any way you can stay home the rest of today?" She looked at the door, then back at her husband. She frowned, and the darkened lashes lowered over her eyes.

"Really, I've had all I can take of that man. Being alone with him . . ."

Whit, his head tipped to one side, examined her face. "I think I'd better stay home," he said. "Alma can take care of things at the library." He put his other hand over hers and patted it. His forehead seemed to ease a little.

John came back to the table. He picked up a green star cookie and broke off its points, rolling them to crumbs between his fingers. "We'd better be thinking of some more things for him to do," he said. "There's the rest of the trim on our house of course, but I haven't really wanted him to do that. I'm not sure he's steady enough to be up on ladders."

"I won't wear my brain out thinking up games for that man," Grace muttered.

Whit rubbed his bald place. "Did you ever get those leather things, John?" he asked.

"Oh, the leather things." John looked tired. "That's right. I was going to pick them up on my lunch hour." The cookie crumbs sifted from his hand and he pushed them into a little hill on the tablecloth. "Well, maybe I can do it after work."

There was a shout from below them and a clatter of feet on the basement stairs. Keith burst into the room, with Betsy just behind him carrying the empty cookie dish. The old cat moved ponderously among their legs.

"Grace!" Keith yelled. "We want more cookies; Hi, Daddy. Hi, Whit."

Ellie reached to touch Keith's dark tumbled hair. He shook off her hand and galloped to the sink counter. Betsy crowded after him. Bumping and giggling, the two of them scooped cookies into the dish.

Ellie sat still. No one was looking at her. All at once she felt as if she were sliding backward, away from them all. They were remote from her. Grace, locked in her resentment, Whit, tense, puttering nervously with his pipe, John. They were all shadows, pictures moving on a screen, and she in the audience watching. Or was she the shadow?

I need you, she cried to them behind silent lips. Cried to them all, to John. Look at me. Look at me. I'm not real when you won't look at me.

Aaron coughed low near her shoulder. She started. He had come in so quietly. "Miz Meade," he said to Grace, "I'll have that coffee now if you don't mind."

Grace stood up stiffly. "All right," she said.

Betsy whirled around from the cookie bowl. "Aaron!" she squealed. She hurled herself at him, hugging his thighs, burying her sugary face against his knees. He stroked her back gently. His hand seemed to tremble less as it touched her.

Ellie's eyes hurt. She stood up and crossed to Aaron, moving with difficulty against the current that wanted to carry her backward. She pried Betsy's hands from him and picked her up. "Betsy needs a rest," she heard herself explain calmly, and felt her mouth smile. "Keith could use one, too. I'll take them home now."

Holding the struggling little girl close to her side with one arm, she took Keith's jacket from the chair where the coats were piled.

"Aw, Mama," Keith complained, "do we have to go home? We were having fun."

"Yes, we have to go home," she told him. Moving smoothly in that shadow world, she buttoned Betsy into her coat and put on her own. "Goodbye," she said, and led the children out the door without looking back.

The slap of icy wind on her face shot her back into life, and into a sudden convulsive sobbing. She pulled the children with her across the street, hoping they did not see her crying, because she did not know how to stop.

Inside the house she dropped their hands and raced down

the hall, slammed her bedroom door, threw herself across the bed, and cried into her pillow soundlessly. After a time, when the crying was done, she rolled over on her back with her arms flung out at her sides, and stared through the window at the bare maple trees and the cold sky.

From far away the front door clicked. Voices in the distance, deep and shrill. Then John was in the bedroom, shutting the door quietly, sitting on the edge of the bed, rubbing his forehead as if it hurt.

She sat up. "John, do we have to keep taking care of him?" she asked. "I'm sorry, I know he needs help, I know you want to help him. But he's so . . ." She shivered.

"I'd rather not have anything more to do with him either," John said. "But I don't see any other way."

She drew her knees up and laced her fingers around them. "John, why was he in solitary confinement? Did he ever tell you?"

"He said it was for hitting a guard. Both times. He was in solitary twice, two different prisons."

"Why did he hit the guards? Were they hurt? John, why was he in prison?" Her voice was shrill now. "Don't you know why he was in prison? Don't any of you know why he was in prison?"

John stood up abruptly, scowling. "I don't know any more than that about it," he flared out. "That was all he told us. He's never said why he was in prison—any of the times he's been there. What do you want from the man, Ellie? A notarized confession?"

Ellie gripped her fingers together until they whitened. "I'm sorry," she said. "I wanted to know."

"Well, that's all I can tell you."

He paced away from her across the room. He slapped the pockets of his suit coat, felt in his shirt pocket. Then he reached for a pack of Ellie's cigarettes on the bureau. He shook one out and lit it, pulling in a long breath. He came back to the bed and sat beside her.

"I'm sorry," he said. "I seem to want to blow up today. Aaron did tell us a little more about himself. After you went home he told us how his marriage finally broke up—and what he was in prison for one time, at least."

"What happened?" she asked, low-voiced.

"Well, you know he married this young girl and they had two children. I don't know where that was, what part of the country. Or how long ago it was. His wife was the daughter of a preacher—one of the hell-fire-and-damnation kind, apparently. She didn't believe in drinking at all. She was always after Aaron to take a pledge. I don't know why she stayed with him as long as she did. Maybe she felt sorry for him."

John got up again and walked restlessly to the window. The ash dropped from his cigarette. He brushed it off his shirt.

"Aaron was drunk just about all the time. He told us he had bottles hidden all over their apartment and buried in the yard. His wife kept finding them and breaking them, but he'd go out and buy more. He was working off and on, and he used all his pay that way."

"What did they live on?"

"Her father gave them money. That is, he gave it to his daughter and the children. He wouldn't have anything to do with Aaron."

John fingered the folds of the window curtain. "His wife didn't see many people outside the family. Aaron was home a lot—he only worked in spurts, the way he does now. Most of the women she knew wouldn't come around when he was there. But she did have one friend, a girl she'd known in high school, who looked in on her every now and then."

He dropped the curtain and pulled his lighter from his pocket, turning it over and over in his hand.

"Aaron would have the D T's sometimes. He would lie in bed and see things. God only knows what kind of things—he couldn't tell us. But he said he would lie there sweating and be too scared to close his eyes. He kept a knife beside him in bed. A big kitchen knife. He thought he could scare the things away with that."

John struck the lighter, watched the flame. Snuffed it out. Lit it again. Snuffed it.

"One time he was lying alone in his bed, watching all the corners of the room, when his wife's friend came to see her. He heard her coming up the stairs to their apartment, and then he saw her shadow by the bedroom door where she stood talking to his wife. He thought it was something come to get him. He grabbed his knife and jumped out of bed. He says he doesn't remember anything after that."

"Oh," Ellie whispered.

"The next thing he remembers is waking up in jail. They told him he'd gone after the girl with his knife. He'd managed to nick her arm before some neighbors got the knife away. They held him while the girl screamed and his wife called a doctor and the police. All the time they held him he was yelling that he'd kill every one of them."

John snapped the lighter shut and put it back in his pocket.

"He was in prison for a long time after that. When he got out his wife was gone. She never lived with him again."

"Oh," Ellie said once more.

She looked down at her fingers. "John, I'm afraid of him," she said. "Can't you take him to the hospital now and commit him? He ought to be in the hospital. You said so yourself. Why do you and Whit have to keep him on?"

"Why?" John's face looked drawn tight. "I don't know why any more. At first it seemed a pretty great thing to do. Now—I just don't know any more. We promised him we wouldn't commit him. I'm not even sure we could do it—we're not relatives. I just don't know."

He paced back to the bed. "If we'd never taken him on in the first place," he said. "If I hadn't gotten myself so involved —but we did. I did. Now somehow we have to see it through." He sank down on the bed and dug his fingers into his scalp. "We have to see it through. Great God, Ellie, it's as if that man is pulling me around on a chain!" His voice rose. "And there's no way to get free of him!"

He let his hands fall to his knees. "Maybe that's what's the matter with me. I have so many goddamn fine ideals. Then life throws a poor wretch like Aaron Sloane at me and says 'here, catch! Show what you believe in!' And right away I want to give up and throw him back."

He slapped his knees with his open palms and stood up. "So we won't commit Aaron to the lock-up," he said. "And I do have to get back to work if I still want a job. Whit's staying home this afternoon. I'll get the leather things and be with Aaron this evening. There isn't anything you need to do about him, Ellie. Maybe you can get some rest—Keith and Betsy are busy with their new Christmas junk."

He opened the bedroom door.

"John?" she asked softly, holding him with her voice. "John, what if it never ends? What if it just goes on and on and he keeps coming back to us? What if we never get rid of him?"

"I don't know," he said. "I'm not thinking past next Thursday morning."

He pulled the door shut after him.

ELEVEN

ELLIE MOVED ABOUT THE GRAY MORNING KITCHEN, RINSING THE coffee pot, laying out bowls and spoons. She hadn't bothered to turn the light on. Her head ached still, with a steady throbbing. She felt as if it had always been aching.

She could no longer even wish she wanted to help Aaron. Her fear of him, unreasoning, shapeless, had spread to fill her sky. Her thinking would not reach as far as Thursday morning. The time between stretched across too blank a void. Besides, she could not believe that Thursday morning, if it ever came, would mean the end of Aaron. He would be theirs forever.

So she moved slowly around the dim room, slowly to slow the time, to keep this small space of morning before she had to tend to the children, before she had to take them to Grace, before there would be Aaron again.

Then she stopped in the middle of the room, a box of corn flakes clutched to her. Of course she couldn't leave her children at the Meades' house.

Grace would take good care of them. Whit would be home all day. They'll all think I'm an idiot, she whispered.

John will think I'm an idiot. Aaron hasn't been dangerous to us.

But she didn't care. Keith and Betsy must not be in the same house with Aaron Sloane. She slammed the cereal box down on the table and ran to the telephone.

As she reached for it, the phone shook to life with a shattering ring. She answered, knowing something had happened.

Grace's voice exploded in her ear. "Ellie, Aaron's gone again. He was gone when we woke up."

Ellie stood motionless, holding the receiver clamped to her ear, not able to understand.

"Ellie? Are you there, Ellie? I said Aaron is gone!"

"I'm here," Ellie said at last. "Aaron's gone?"

"He must have left sometime in the night. He took his things, what things he had."

Ellie sank limply down on a chair. Could this be the end of it, then? Grace's voice still rose and fell in her ear. She struggled to divide the textured sound into words.

". . . and I just don't know what he'll do, Ellie. He said such things to Whit last night. Ellie, I'm really afraid. I just don't . . ."

"Afraid?" Ellie broke in. "Grace, do we still have to be afraid? He's gone, you said. You said he took his things. Why are you afraid?"

"You don't understand, Ellie." The voice rose sharply. "He is gone—he doesn't want to stay any more and right now he doesn't need to stay. But he'll come back. I'm sure he will. Whit says he will. The minute he needs . . . Ellie, he knows those men of ours will take him in. He'll come back. Oh, you don't know what he was saying last night. You weren't here."

No, she hadn't been there last night. John had gone over after a hurriedly swallowed dinner and had stayed until past midnight. Ellie had read the children several chapters of

Winnie the Pooh, had bathed them and put them to bed. She had washed the dishes. She had put away the toys scattered over the living room, replaced burnt-out Christmas tree bulbs, sorted through the magazines on the end table, dusted the leaves of the philodendron plant on the windowsill.

She had stood at the window for a long moment, staring across the empty street.

She had filled the bathtub deep with steaming water and a few drops of the perfume John had given her for her birthday. She had soaked until the fragrant water felt part of her skin, or her skin part of the water.

She had put on a flame-colored robe and had taken two aspirins. She had brought the last of the gin down from the attic and had made herself a Tom Collins with the one withered lemon hiding at the back of the refrigerator.

At last she had fallen into bed, and—late—had been lifted only to the misty fringe of awareness when John had crawled silently in beside her.

"What was Aaron saying last night?" she asked now into the telephone.

"He was terrible," Grace said. "Just terrible. He couldn't sit still, and he looked worse all the time, and he kept on talking about the lock-up and begging Whit and John not to make him go there. He begged them over and over—even after they'd promised they wouldn't make him go. Then Ellie, it must have been just a little bit before John went home —he looked around at all of us, slow, that way he does sometimes, you know, and he said 'I think I'd kill anybody if they wanted to put me in that lock-up.' And, Ellie, it might sound crazy, but somehow the way he said that, I think . . . I almost think he'd do it."

"Oh," Ellie said weakly.

"Anyway, we all just feel he'll come back, and there's no telling when. Whit's staying home today, of course. I'm afraid to be alone here. I don't know, Ellie, the way Aaron is right now, if he got drunk I think he might try to . . . even if he just thought somebody was going to put him in the lock-up, even if they weren't really going to—he might . . ." She let the sentence hang, unfinished.

Ellie heard water running in the bathroom, Keith and Betsy murmuring in sleepy morning voices. "Grace," she said quickly, "tell Whit I've got to stay home today, too. I can't leave the children. I have to be with them."

The hammering in her skull had sharpened. "Maybe he won't come back, Grace," she said, not believing it.

"Oh, I hope he won't," Grace cried. "I'll tell Whit you're not going in. He'll understand. Goodbye, now. I'll talk to you later."

"Goodbye."

Slowly, Ellie replaced the receiver and came back to the kitchen. She rested her elbows on the edge of the sink and rubbed her throbbing head.

The day dragged. John went to work late and called home every few hours to check up. Ellie locked the doors and wandered aimlessly around the house, watching the children, drinking cup after cup of black coffee.

Aaron did not call.

Whit and Grace came over after dinner. The four of them sat making vacant conversation, listening, trying not to listen for the ring of the telephone, the sound of the doorbell.

Whit's eyes were red-veined, the skin around them pink. "Aaron still has my glasses," he explained apologetically. "It's been rather hard to read without them."

Grace's lips thinned and tightened when he said it.

Thursday morning came and passed. Ellie stayed home again, guarding her children, or hiding with them. Whit went to the library for a few hours, then waited at home with Grace. John quit work early in the afternoon.

"How long was he gone the other time?" Grace asked on Thursday evening.

"Just overnight, wasn't it?" John said. "He took off right after Christmas dinner, and then it was the next morning when Whit got that note."

Grace studied her watch as if it could tell her more than the time. "It's been a lot longer than that, now," she observed.

By Friday afternoon the air in the house was oppressive. Ellie felt the walls stifle her. Aaron had never called. The fear that had kept her hiding for three days began to seem a child's fear.

"Bogeymen again," she told herself sourly, finding coats and caps, tugging mittens over small fingers. "How stupid can you get, Ellie Clark?" The children raced ahead of her out of the house.

She stood a moment on the step, swallowing deep grateful breaths of the cold air. The late-afternoon sky was majestic with clouds, mountains of cumulus, grays over grays. Pearl colors, seagull colors. Snow clouds, perhaps. The hugeness of them eased her—beneath them she felt herself expand. She started off behind the children, realizing only now in the loosening of fear how afraid she had been. Of poor, dreary Aaron Sloane.

The Meade's door opened across the street. Grace's head poked out, Grace's arm gestured widely. "Ellie! Yoo-hoo, Ellie! Bring the kids over—I've got some fresh cinnamon rolls!"

Keith charged across the street with a shout. Betsy galloped after him. Ellie followed, climbing to the wide front porch.

"Grace, I just have to be outside for a while," she said. "I've been cooped up so long in that house like an idiot. I thought I'd walk some—may the kids stay with you?"

"Oh, of course," said Grace. "I wouldn't have them miss these rolls while they're hot out of the oven. You just take your time, Ellie. Stop by later if you can."

"Thanks, Grace."

Back to the sidewalk, walking into the seagull clouds.

On the street beside her a brilliant red Volkswagon growled to a pause, its motor ticking gently.

"Hey" A face craned out of the car's window; a grinning, square face, blue eyes squinting with the grin beneath a blond curve of hair.

"You're—uh—Ellie, aren't you? I met you a few days ago, with my aunt. I'm Byron Richardson."

Wilma Kirkland's nephew. Ellie stopped. "Yes, I'm Ellie. Ellie Clark." She smiled, happy to see him. "How's your vacation going?"

"It's going." He made a face. "Aunt Wilma's running me off my feet, hauling me all over town, showing me off. All her friends that haven't seen me since I was so high." He gestured, his hand held low through the window of the little car. "I'm starting to feel like a prize hog. I can see why my cousin stays gone."

Ellie laughed. "Is it that bad?" she asked.

"Worse sometimes. Well, you must know Aunt Wilma." He pushed the blond wave up from his forehead. "I kind of like it, though. She and Uncle George are pretty great. And I could get used to being the star attraction. But I couldn't take it twenty-four hours a day. Aunt Wilma wanted me to stay with them, but I told her I have to have a place to get away to when I need it. So I'm in a motel. Figured I knew what it was going to be like here, and I sure was right."

"You were smart."

"Yeah, I guess. Well, I'm about late—Aunt Wilma has some dinner party she's giving—more old friends I've got to meet."

He pushed the gear shift into first. "Oh, Ellie, you'll be at that New Year's party they're having tomorrow, won't you?" His eyes caught hers with the same attentive look they had held before. "I'll see you there." He drove away, grinning back at her, waving a square hand.

"Goodbye!" she called.

Once again, unreasonably, she was glad he hadn't asked if she were married. Glad she had been alone. She walked on, keeping the look he'd given her, saving it for no purpose, like a gardenia pressed in a high school yearbook.

She thought about the Kirkland's party, looking forward to it. George and Wilma gave their enormous New Year's party every winter. Their house, the long brick one at the end of the block, would be shimmering with colored lights, choked with food, with music, with people.

The people. Always more people than ought to be possible, jamming the L-shaped living room, spilling into the study, the kitchen, the hall. Faces, appearing, vanishing. Voices, shouting above the hi-fi's beat. Old friends, acquaintances barely known, strangers, blended and poured together in a kaleidoscopic tumbling of people.

Always she and John dragged home exhausted in the cold early hours of the New Year—feet aching from the standing, throats raw from the shouting, heads that felt stuffed with foam rubber. Too much to eat, too much to drink. Too many people too fast too shiftingly. Too many words said and heard. Too few words given or understood. And yet always fun. Always something to think of with a touch of pleasure, of expectancy.

Ellie felt the expectancy now. And then, underneath the expectancy, the shapeless form of fear returning.

In the evening, with dinner on the table, she lingered at the sink. She took a cigarette from the pack on the window sill, lighted it, watched the smoke bloom. "The Kirklands are having their party tomorrow," she said to John. The expectancy. Even larger, the fear.

"Oh Lord. Tomorrow?"

John looked tired. A few hairs had separated from his thick eyebrows and swirled upward like dark question marks. "About the last thing I feel like doing is fighting my way through that screeching crowd at the Kirklands'. But I guess George'd be hurt if we didn't go. I don't see how in God's name he keeps track of who's at those mob scenes of his, but he always knows."

Ellie pushed her finger through a drop of water on the counter, spreading it into a star, a square, drawing it out in a streak. "I was wondering if we really ought to be away from home—away from the children," she said. "If we did hear from Aaron . . ." She left the sentence unfinished.

John was mashing butter into Betsy's baked potato. "You've got Susie Atkins lined up to sit, haven't you?" he asked. "She'd call us. The Kirklands only live down the street."

Ellie twirled the water back into a circle. "I feel sort of funny about it, that's all," she said. "Susie's not more than fifteen. And Aaron's so . . . oh, you know how he is." She mashed the cigarette in the sink and left it there.

Without warning John stood up. His chair banged back against the wall. "Ellie, right now I'm good and damn sick of your feeling funny about things," he said. His voice was harsh. "The Kirkland's party isn't all that important, but what do you want to do? Stay in a locked-up house the rest of your life because you have a funny feeling? Of course Aaron could show up tomorrow night. My God. Or he might show up in two weeks or two months. Or there might be a tornado or a nuclear attack or the sky might cave in. Why don't you just dig a hole in the ground and hide in it with your funny feelings and be completely safe?"

130

Ellie stood still, her eyes locked on him. The other fear, the fear of Aaron, shrank before his anger. "I guess we'd better go to the party," she said.

And then wondered suddenly whether it was her fear he fought, or his own.

He took a breath that just missed being a snort. "You're damn right we'll go to the party," he said.

On Saturday afternoon it snowed. Keith and Betsy raced outside, shrieking in triumph, when the first white specks blew out of a darkened sky. The snow came steadily thicker; first flake by flake, then speckling the yard, then dropping in a heavy mesh through which the trees and houses seemed to float upward.

When the ground was blanketed Ellie pulled a fluff-lined jacket over her slacks and sweater, covered her hair rollers with a red scarf, dug boots out of the coat closet, and opened the door on a snow-silent world.

She stood on the step, feeling the motion of snow that seemed the motion of the earth. Snow enveloped her, whirling away any thought, any fear, any life apart from itself.

She pulled the clean air, needle-sharp, deep into her lungs and ran through the world of shining flakes to tag the children. She gathered heaps of snow in her mittens and threw them at the maple tree, at the shrouded car, at the white-dusted bright berries of the bitter-sweet vine.

When she came in, stamping snow from her boots, her cheeks were burning with cold and her mouth was stiffened in the shape of laughter. John was stretched in the easy chair with a book on his knees. She bent to kiss his forehead, hot under her cold lips, and ran a snowy mitten around the back of his neck and under his collar.

"Yeouch!" he yelled. He jerked forward, shaking her off. "What are you trying to do, woman?"

"Chicken!" she taunted. "Come on outside. Snowballs at ten paces.

He grinned and pulled himself out of the chair. "You'll live to regret that," he threatened.

He was fastening his plaid wool jacket when the telephone's bell shrilled into the room. He leaned over and picked up the receiver. "John Clark," he said. He frowned. "Yes, I'll accept it."

Listening idly, Ellie pulled her mittens off and slapped them together. Melted snow spattered from them to freckle the rug around her feet.

"I can hardly hear you," John was saying. "Oh . . ." He was silent for a long time.

Ellie peered out the diamond-shaped pane of glass in the door. Keith and Betsy were holding up mittened hands, catching snowflakes. She looked back at John. He had turned away from her, leaning an arm against the wall, the receiver propped to his ear.

"Where did you say you are, Aaron?" he asked.

Aaron. Ellie sank down on the couch, forgetting the snow on her clothes. She brought reddened fingertips to her mouth.

"I'm sorry that's the way it is," John said into the telephone. "I am sorry. But we've done all we know how . . ." There was another long silence.

"I see," John said at last. "Well, I'm not sure what you think we can do . . ."

He shifted around, leaning his back against the wall. "Mound Hill . . . yes . . . I understand. No, I'll find you."

He replaced the receiver and sat down by the telephone. "You heard that," he said heavily.

"Aaron wants to come back," said Ellie. "And you are going to take him back."

John rubbed his eyelids. "He's in Mound Hill. Very sick. He woke up in some shack out in the slum district a little

132

while ago and found his way to the bus station. God knows how he got that far."

"I didn't know Mound Hill had a slum district," Ellie said. "I didn't think the town was big enough."

Aaron Sloane could find a slum anywhere." John's mouth twisted. "If there wasn't one before, he'd start his own."

Ellie chewed the side of her thumb. "John," she said, "it's fifteen miles to Mound Hill. And it's snowing hard."

"I'll have to put the chains on," he said.

He watched the snow swirl against the window. "Ellie, he says if he steps outside the bus station he'll get picked up by the first cop that sees him. And I suppose he's right. I have to bring him back here. Let him spend the night and clean up and get through his hangover. No more than that. I just can't throw him out . . . without giving him that much chance, at least." He rested his forehead in his hands.

"I see," Ellie said dully.

Slowly she got up and walked around John to the telephone. "I'll tell Susie we won't need her to sit this evening."

"I suppose you'd better," he said.

TWELVE

ELLIE HALF-SAT, HALF-KNELT ON THE COUCH, STARING OUT THE black window behind it, willing her sight to cut through the blackness, willing John to get home.

The dark was a solid thing. It blotted out the street, the houses, trees, everything there was. Even the snow drifted down unseen, except where isolated pools of light picked it out. A fringe of snow glistened just beyond the window glass; farther out the street light's blue-white cone trapped briefly a dense moving curtain that dropped from blackness, fell to blackness.

More than two hours now since John had left for Mound Hill. Could it take so long?

But the snow. But the solid dark.

Her eyes, tired from reaching into the night, loosened their focus. The warm lighted living room reflected in the glass was easier to look at. The night beyond the window grayed its colors, but still they were colors.

There was the Christmas tree, the table. The faded easy chair. The television flickering its sterile passions. Betsy and Keith in front of it, curled on the rug, watching. Greens and blues and reds from the Christmas bulbs painted Keith's cheek, Betsy's soft-tangled hair.

Nearer, larger in the window, Ellie's own face resting on her wrist. A pale, big-eyed face, lips wide, chin a little pointed. She had taken out her hair rollers and had done her hair the way she would have worn it for the party. It had been something to do while she waited. The hair waved back deeply from her forehead, the smooth bun was replaced with a sweeping twist.

She'd never tried that kind of twist before. It made her someone different. She turned her face to the side, studying the unfamiliar shape. It would have looked nice with the black sheath. The party would have been fun.

Well, which is more important—parties or people?

Still, it would have been fun. Wilma's nephew would be there. Byron Richardson. It would have been fun to come in with John and see him, she thought. He never asked if I was married. I never said anything to make him think I might be. Why didn't I?

Maybe he wouldn't have looked at me the way he did if he'd known I was married. Any woman would like being looked at that way.

I'd come in and Byron would see me and I'd introduce him to John. And maybe . . . Byron might be sorry I'm married. And maybe . . . if he saw that, John might be jealous.

No. No.

You don't need jealousy from John, Ellie Clark. That isn't what you want from him. Is it? Isn't it enough to have his love? Or can't you believe you have his love?

Twin tubes of snow-filled light streaked the darkness beyond her ghostly face, turned toward her, shortening to yellow circles, and stopped. The Plymouth—John was home. And Aaron.

135

She eased herself stiffly from the couch. She held the front door open and switched on the outside light.

John climbed out of the car first. He trudged around to the other door, pulled it open, and helped Aaron out. Aaron stood a moment in the snow, shaking his head, then stumbled ahead of John to the house. The light fell harshly on his stubbled face, sharpening its skeletal ridges and hollows. He was wearing John's overcoat again.

He didn't look at Ellie, but wavered past her into the house and on down the hall to the bedroom he had used before.

Betsy bounced up from her place before the television set. She would have run after Aaron, but Ellie caught her and held her close until he was out of sight. "Don't bother him now, honey," she whispered. "He doesn't feel good."

John closed the door behind him, leaning against it. "God, what a trip," he said. "Roads were terrible. I had to keep it under thirty the whole way there and back. Couldn't have made it at all without the chains."

"How is he?" Ellie moved her head in the direction of the hall.

"He's in bad shape. He was waiting for me in the bus station—it's really just part of a little all-night grocery store there in Mound Hill. He was sitting on a chair back of some crates and things—trying to keep from being noticed too much, I guess. I've never seen him so filthy. He'd been sick— it was all over his clothes. I gave him my coat to cover up the filth as much as to keep him warm. He'd lost his own coat again, of course."

"Did you tell him he'd have to leave in the morning?"

John's eyes shifted to the black window. "I haven't talked to him much yet. Just brought him home. I thought we could talk when he's feeling better."

He scowled. "Great God, Ellie, it's all the poor bastard can do to stand up right now, let alone talk."

"I just wondered," Ellie said.

The door behind John opened a crack and Whit's face pushed through. His forehead crinkled with anxiety. "May I come in?" he asked. "John, how is he? Ellie called me."

John turned and opened the door the rest of the way. "He's godawful, thank you," he said.

Betsy broke away from her mother and tackled Whit around the knees. "Aaron come home!" she squealed excitedly.

Whit patted her hair. He laid his coat over the arm of the couch. "Grace and I were talking about this," he said. "John, Grace doesn't think we ought to fool around with Aaron any more, you know, letting him stay here."

"I'm not about to let him stay here," John said crisply. "He's out first thing in the morning. I'm just giving him a chance to clean up and get his feet under him so he won't be arrested first thing. After that he's on his own."

Whit's forehead wrinkled more deeply. "Well, I'll go along with that, John," he said. "But do you think we ought to put him out on the street in the morning? Grace felt we should really insist on taking him to the hospital tomorrow. Make that the condition for his staying here tonight."

"The lock-up?" John asked.

Whit nodded. "The lock-up." His voice sounded scratchy.

Ellie moved closer to John. Her arm touched his sleeve. "Whit, you know how Aaron feels about the lock-up," she said.

Again Whit nodded. The skin of his face seemed yellowed. "I know," he said. "But Grace still thought we should put the hospital on a take-it-or-leave-it basis. And if he wouldn't agree to the hospital, well he just couldn't stay here."

137

He cleared his throat. "I do have a sort of idea for getting him through the night."

John eased into his chair. "What is it?" he asked.

"Well, it's a technique the AA uses sometimes. I've helped out with it before. We actually give Aaron whiskey, in measured doses. An ounce every two hours, I think it is."

"All night?" John wanted to know.

"All night. We'd have to sit up with him. Possibly you and I could take turns. It sounds like the opposite of what we've been doing till now, but it can help when a man's in as bad shape as Aaron is. The idea is to wean him, you might say, when it's too much of a shock to him to sober up all at once. But we wouldn't have to complete the weaning. Just get him through the night and into the hospital."

John's eyebrows pulled together. "Well, we could suggest it to him." he said doubtfully. "It does seem to make sense. I would like to get him to the hospital tomorrow. I'd feel that we'd finished what we started, if we did that."

Keith looked up from the television, for the first time aware of his father and Whit. "Hey, that was a real good show, Daddy," he said. "There was this thing, kind of, that lived under the ocean, and whenever it came out . . ."

"Not now, Keithy." Ellie waved him to silence. "Tell us about it later."

"Well, can we watch 'Agent 76'? It's just starting."

"Shhh. Go ahead and watch it."

"Oh boy!" Keith squealed. "C'mon, Betsy, we get to watch this whole next one!" He squirmed closer to the flickering eye of the set, his chin propped on his two fists.

"Where is he now?" Whit asked.

"Keith's room," John said. "Come on."

Ellie followed the two or them mutely.

Aaron was lying on Keith's bed, the brown cowboy spread wrinkled under him. When he saw them he sat up care-

138

fully. Painfully, it seemed to Ellie. He wore a bathrobe of John's that Ellie had laid out for him. His legs poked out from it, stick-like, matted with hairs. His face was blotched with red, his forehead twisted in a network of furrows. The gray-speckled hair lay greasy on the back of his neck, and gray bristles spoked out over his cheeks and chin. His clothes and John's overcoat lay in a heap on the floor.

There was a rank smell in the room. It spread through Ellie's lungs. She found herself taking shallow breaths, as if in that way she could be free from it.

John hiked himself up on top of Keith's low bureau. He sat there swinging his legs, looking casual. More casual than he ever really looks, Ellie thought.

"See here, Aaron," he said. "You do need help, and Whit and I want to help you. But we've all been wondering whether it is helping you, just letting you stay on here."

"We think it might be too much for you," Whit put in, "in your—the way you are now—to wait until the alcoholic center would take you."

Aaron's colorless eyes watched them silently from the bed.

John shifted his weight. "You need to be in the regular hospital, Aaron," he said. "We think that's the only chance you have. I know you don't like the idea, but . . ."

"We'd let you have whiskey tonight," Whit interrupted. "A little bit every two hours—that's how the AA does it sometimes. The night wouldn't be so hard for you that way, you see. And then in the morning we would drive you over to Cedarville. If you agreed."

"I'm afraid there isn't anything more we can do for you if you won't go along with this arrangement, Aaron," said John. His voice was steady, but Ellie saw his hands grip and whiten on the edge of the bureau. She left a stab of pain in her knuckle and realized she had been biting it.

Still Aaron watched them all, saying nothing.

139

John pushed himself down from the bureau. "That's the only help we can give you," he said. "If you don't want it, we'll drive you downtown right now and let you off wherever you like. You can't stay with us tonight unless you'll go to the hospital tomorrow."

Aaron grunted and stretched back on the bed. He threw an arm over his face, covering his eyes. "I'll try the hospital," he said.

"I'll never understand him," said Whit when they were all back in the living room. "He didn't even argue. After all that talk about the lock-up the other night."

John stared moodily at the Christmas tree. "He's stopped fighting it," he said. "In a way it almost seems sad. Well, I'd better go up in the attic and see how the liquor supply's holding out."

Ellie shook herself into action and stepped forward to turn off the television, lift Keith from his place in front of it, and propel him to the bathroom and his pajamas. Then she came back for Betsy, fallen asleep in a small warm huddle on the floor. She carried her to bed and tucked her under the covers without undressing her.

Keith's head was drooping as he worked with buttons and zippers. Ellie helped him finish and led him to the folding cot in Betsy's room. He hunched up under the blankets and ground his face into the pillow. Then one half-open gray eye peered out at her. "Good show coming on now," he mumbled.

"No," she told him.

The eye drifted shut before he could complain.

When she came back to the living room John was pulling on his coat. "We were almost out of whiskey," he said. "Didn't look as if there was enough up there to last the night. I've got the chains on, so I'm going out to get some more before the stores close."

Ellie's eyes jumped anxiously toward the hall. Whit caught

the look. He gave her a smile that did nothing to smooth the worried lines of his forehead.

"I'll be here," he assured her. "I'll give him his first dose. And Grace will be over pretty soon. She just had a few things to finish up at home first."

John was sliding his fingers into heavy leather gloves. "Aaron!" he called. "I'm going to buy you some more whiskey. I'll be right back."

A croaking voice sounded from Keith's room.

"What did you say?" John shouted. He trudged down the hall, awkward in snow boots.

When he came back his mouth was a stiff line. "He wants Hiram Walker Ten High bourbon," he said. "Hundred proof. As long as I was going out anyway." He left, and the door slammed behind him.

Whit shook his head. "Well, I'd better get his first dose into him," he said.

Ellie followed Whit to the kitchen. She didn't want to be left by herself. When he carried the partly filled shot glass and a glass of water in to Aaron, she was right behind.

Aaron sat up in bed, his pale eyes fixed on the shot glass. He reached out a trembling hand to take it. He tipped his head back and poured the bourbon into his mouth all in a gulp. Coughing violently, he handed the glass to Whit. Whit gave him the water. He sipped at it while the coughing subsided. Then he put the water glass on Keith's bedside table and sat quietly on the edge of the bed; just sat, staring ahead. His shoulders slumped loose and his hands rested in his lap.

Ellie looked at his eyes. Pink and pale and wet eyes. Dead eyes suddenly. It was as if they had gone out, all at once, like turning off a light. Dead eyes with nothing alive behind them. They might have been painted on a Hallowe'en mask. Would it be much different when the rest of him was dead? She shivered.

"Do you think you could sleep now, Aaron?" Whit asked softly.

Aaron curled down on the bed like an obedient child.

"What's the matter with him, Whit?" Ellie whispered when they were back in the kitchen. "You only gave him an ounce. Did you see his eyes?"

Whit looked anxious. "I don't know," he said. "Something happens to the brain sometimes—with people who have been alcoholic as long as Aaron has."

He ran a hand up his forehead and back to the fringe of hair. "Do you know, Ellie, that first time he came back—maybe four beers really was all he'd had."

They sat at the table. Ellie poured coffee, steaming and strong, into squat black mugs. She liked the mugs. They seemed to make the coffee more cheering. All of them needed cheering tonight.

Then Grace pushed through the back door carrying a tray of warm sugar cookies. Her hair quivered in a stiff cluster of sausage curls, and her mouth was set hard. She thumped the tray down on the table and tossed her coat over the back of a chair. "I'm here," she announced. "Well, let's hope tonight's the last we spend with that man."

They sat and drank the coffee, cup after cup of it, and munched the sweet crumbling cookies, and kept looking at the clock on the kitchen wall.

Twice Whit went to the door of Keith's room.

"Still asleep," he reported the first time.

Later, "He's awake, but he just groaned and rolled over when he saw me."

At last John came back, stamping snow from his boots, a slender brown bag clutched in one hand. Snow melted on his eyebrows and in the dark hair over his forehead. "It's like the South Pole out there," he said. "How's our friend?"

"Be careful, John," Grace laughed. Her laugh was almost

savage, all tenderness gone from it. "He'll smell that stuff right through the bottle and be in here like a streak."

John folded himself into a chair and slid his arms out of his wet coat. "We all may need the old AA treatment before this night's over," he said. "But I'll start out with coffee, Ellie, if there's any left in the pot."

"Lots. And I'll put on more." She filled one of the big mugs and set it in front of him. "When does he get his next dose, Whit?"

"About eleven." Whit looked at his watch. "Another hour, almost."

"Does anybody know why we're doing this?" Grace asked.

"What else could we do?" Whit stared dismally into his mug.

"We took him on," John said. "If we'd told him to go to hell in the first place . . . but we took him on."

"Maybe he would have been better off if we had turned him away in the first place," Grace mused. "I know it would have been better for us if we had. But if he can keep on sponging off people he'll never change."

John poured a thin line of cream into his coffee. "I don't think I could have turned him away then," he said. "I don't think you could have, either, Whit."

For a time no one spoke.

Then a quavering groan sounded down the hall, a thud and a shuffle of feet, and Aaron came in. He stood in the kitchen doorway, swaying and clinging to the door frame. His feet were bare. Dirt crusted them. The toenails were thick and yellow and needed cutting. Aaron had been so careful to be clean, before.

"Time yet?" he mumbled. His eyes were squeezed to slits. "Would you let me have more whiskey?"

Whit went to him. "It won't be long now, Aaron," he said. "I want you to wait just a little longer. We have to do this on schedule." He cupped a hand under Aaron's elbow and guided him back to the bedroom.

As soon as the hands of the kitchen clock touched eleven John opened the bottle he had brought in. He measured an ounce into the shot glass and took it to Keith's room. The others came silently, in procession, after him.

John sat at the foot of the bed while Aaron drained the glass. "Does it help?" he asked.

Aaron nodded, coughing. "Couldn't have stood it, without," he muttered when he could speak. Again the reddened eyes were without life.

John walked over to the bureau. He leaned against it uneasily and watched the man slumped on the edge of the bed.

"Aaron," he said suddenly, "how do I know you won't come in some time during the night and bang me on the head and take that bottle?"

Ellie's knuckle fled to her mouth.

Aaron turned the extinguished eyes toward John. "What do you think I am?" he asked.

John looked at him steadily. "I don't know what you are, Aaron Sloane," he said.

Aaron lay back and bunched the blankets over himself. "Won't hurt you," he mumbled.

John kept on. It was as if he had to. "There's nothing to stop you if you want that bottle badly enough," he said.

Aaron grunted. The papery eyelids dropped and he was quiet.

All at once the room, the bed, the rancid air were more than Ellie could bear. The floor heaved under her. She ran to the kitchen and pulled a glass from the cupboard. She poured some bourbon into it from Aaron's bottle. She swallowed the whiskey quickly, straight as it came from the bottle, letting it sear her throat and burn its way to her stomach. Then she poured a little more into the glass and added a squirt of water from the tap. She stood by the sink and sipped the drink, feeling the floor grow steady beneath her feet, the ice inside her begin to melt.

As she emptied the glass she heard a pounding on the front step. The doorbell shrilled. She wandered to the front door.

George Kirkland was standing there on the step. Nice George Kirkland, like a friendly bear in his heavy coat. Grinning, red-cheeked, blinking kindly at her from behind round snowy glasses.

"Come in, George, I'm glad to see you," she said, meaning it.

George shook himself, showering snow. "Where in the hell have you and John been?" he boomed. "Been waiting for you ever since that party got going. Anything the matter over here?"

Ellie smiled and put her finger to her lips. "Shh," she warned him. "I guess we can't make it to this one, George. John and Whit Meade have been taking care of this alcoholic, you know—he's back in Keith's room now and he's in pretty bad shape."

George whistled. "Alcoholic, huh? Relative of yours?"

"No," she said. "Just a man who came to us for help. They're sitting up with him tonight, giving him whiskey every two hours. So he'll hold out till they can get him over to Cedarville in the morning. It's supposed to be an AA treatment."

"Great God and little fishes!" George whistled again. "Well, everybody's got to be a saint once, I guess, and get it out of his system. Good luck!"

He turned to leave, then paused on the step. "We'll be going strong at our place for a long time yet," he said. "If you do get a chance to come over it'd be great to have you. Or if you want to shake old John and come on by yourself. Whole town's there, damn near. But we missed you folks."

"We'll see how things work out," she said. She closed the door after him, and stood a moment looking at it.

Nice people. Really nice. Their world was so simple. George's small variety store—no huge success, no great failure. Wilma. The two of them loved each other. They liked their friends, let them be whatever they wanted to be—even saints. Does life have to be so difficult?

She went on down the hall. Aaron was sitting up now, with the checkerboard on his lap. He was arranging a pile of burnt matches into patterns on the board.

As Ellie came in he swept the matchsticks together, shaking his head. "Just wait," he said. "I'll get it right this next time. It's a real good trick."

John and Whit hovered by the bed, watching him. Grace was sitting on Keith's low chair. She looked resigned.

Aaron bent over the checkerboard, his tongue poking out over his lower lip. "Bet you never saw anything like this," he said.

"John," Ellie said, low. "Come here just a minute, will you?" She tugged at his arm. Reluctantly he followed her into the hall.

"Is it important?" he asked. "Aaron's starting to feel a little better, I think. He's been showing us some match tricks."

Ellie shrugged. "I guess it's not very important," she said. "George Kirkland was just over to see why we weren't at the party. I told him about Aaron, of course. But John, after he left I was wondering—couldn't we take turns with Grace and Whit, maybe, and go over there just for a while?"

"Oh El." he said, "that thing at the Kirkland's is nothing but a giant traffic jam." The line was deep between his heavy brows. "I know Aaron's no fun for you. He's no picnic for any of us. But whether he is or not, what we're doing for him tonight is the last thing we can do for him. If we can keep him calm enough so he'll be able to stick it out and get in that hospital, then we'll have given him what he really needs at last. He'll be taken care of."

"John, he's so terrible," she whispered. "And you'll never get him to that hospital. Something will happen, I know it. Or if you do get him there he'll find some way to come back to us. He makes us do whatever he wants us to do."

"Maybe he did play us for suckers before," he said. "But now we're using some sense, I think." Frowning, he studied her face. "This is life, Ellie. People aren't always grateful and loving when you help them. Sometimes they can be damn disgusting. But that doesn't mean they don't need help. And it doesn't give you an excuse not to do what you can for them."

"Oh John, no!" It was a fierce whisper. Her fists were clenched tight. In spite of the bourbon everything in her was knotted tight. "He knows how to work you. He does what he wants with all of us. He'll come back and back and back— he won't ever be gone! Oh John . . ."

"Ellie, can't you grow up?" He looked at her bleakly. "You were like a child when I married you, but I thought you might grow up eventually. You never did. God help me, I don't suppose you ever will."

He turned and walked away from her, back to Aaron, leaving her alone with his words.

"No no no no," she whispered.

She went to their own room and stretched out on the big double bed. She stared at the opaque ceiling. "No," she said again.

The room, the house rang with John's words. She squeezed her eyes shut, closing out his words, his eyes. She floated away, once again a shadow in a shadow world. Unreal.

But the bourbon warmed her, and suddenly it was almost

pleasant, not being real. Nothing could touch her. She let the shadows drift around her, never touching.

Then her eyes flew open and she sat up. All at once, in sharp panic, she wanted to be real. She wanted to touch, to feel, to live—to hate if that were necessary. To be real.

She never did anything. She never decided anything. John did, always. And now it was Aaron Sloane, deciding for them all.

Move, her mind shouted. Get out. Go anywhere, do anything—cut through the shadows. Before it's too late. Before the shadows seal you in forever.

A scream began inside her, but she jumped from the bed and did not scream it.

She ran to her dresser and looked at herself in the mirror. The carefully sprayed and twisted hair had loosened only a little. She poked an extra pin in here and there, and dashed on fresh lipstick. She took a longer time lining her eyes, brushing her lashes with mascara. Then she stood back from the mirror and looked up and down her small figure. Slacks and sweater? Well, it didn't matter that much. And she was in a hurry. Not knowing exactly why, she had to hurry.

She tiptoed past Keith's door, down the hall, to the coat closet in the living room. She pulled out her fleecy red jacket and slid into it. She shoved her feet into the white boots, still wet from the afternoon. She tied a long wool scarf around her head and flopped the dangling ends of it behind her shoulders.

"John," she called. "I'm going over to the Kirklands'." And was out the door and into the drifted snow before he had time to answer.

THIRTEEN

SNOW WAS STILL FALLING IN THE DARK. SHE RAN THROUGH IT, jumping the drifts. When she reached the buried sidewalk she slowed. She lifted her face to the pelting flakes, let them burn on her cheeks, her tongue. Felt her feet sink in the snow, felt it pack under her boots as she stepped it down. With her running, with the freezing air in her lungs, a frantic anger had filled her. Senseless anger. She tried to reason with it—He'll be gone in the morning. He can't manage to stay on this time. Not this time. They know what they're doing this time. They won't let him stay. It's just for tonight. Only tonight.

But they let him come back tonight. They've let him come back before. No matter what they've said, they've always let him come back. All he's ever had to do was ask.

It's different now.

Are you sure?

The anger in her swelled and shook like a fist at all her world. She kicked the snow as she walked, spraying it out in a half-seen fountain.

Hate Aaron Sloane . . . hate him . . . hate him . . . hate him . . . A furious harsh whisper to the rhythm of her crunching boots—"Hate every one of them. All clustered around him like ants around honey. For all their talk about being firm. Ants!"

She scooped a handful of snow and hurled it at the spectral trunk of a tree.

None of them ever cared how I felt. None of them care now. It's all Aaron Aaron Aaron, that damn parasite Aaron.

Oh, they like me, maybe. But I don't interest them, I'm not a smelly old drunk. Damn!

Another handful of snow, flung murderously against the cold wind.

Well, you know you could go along with them. Grace goes along with them. She's fed up, but she goes along. You don't have to stay on the outside.

"Damned if I'll join them!" she shouted into the snow. "Them and their smelly old drunk!"

She walked faster, kicking snow ahead of her.

If they were ants around honey, she was worse. She was a fly on the edge of a spider web. Hating the spider, scared of the spider, but caught on the sticky threads, not able to get away.

Caught on the edge watching. Trapped in the shadows watching. Always the watcher.

You can't stay on the edges forever, Ellie Clark. Join the rest of them or else get away. Somehow, anyhow, get away.

Well, it wouldn't kill you to go back and join them now. Not for Aaron Sloane. For them. For John.

"No!" She fired the word defiantly. "No, no, no, no!"

The Kirkland's house loomed in the darkness, every window golden. A beat of music drifted from it, muffled, only the deep tone sounding. The New Year's party. Just a big traffic jam, John had said. Nothing so great to do. Nothing so great to stay home from. Not all that important. But a place to get away to.

She ran over churned snow to the wreathed and lighted front door. Do something, get off the edges, anything to get off the edges.

Wilma Kirkland opened the door to her ring. "Ellie!" she exclaimed. She hugged Ellie swiftly. "We didn't think you were going to make it. It's such a wonderful party this year. John's coming?" Her grin pulled her lips back from the big, gum-bordered front teeth.

"It looks like a good party," Ellie said. She gave Wilma her coat and scarf, stooped to pull off her boots.

"Go right on in the living room, dear. Get somebody to fix you a drink. Food's in the dining room." Wilma's firm hand on her back steered her into the party.

Then Wilma was gone and she was engulfed by people. Too many people, an ocean of people. Faces. No identities, just meaningless collections of parts. Noses in a fantasy assortment. Mouths—thick, narrow, pale, lip-sticked—moving and moving, obscenely moving. Acres of damp pink satin. Eyes eyes eyes eyes . . .

Smells—sweet thick sharp musky flowery spice smoke grease wax choking . . .

She gulped air. She was a child alone in a crowded place, a crowd of eyes and none of them seeing her . . . What if I can't breathe? What if there's not enough air? Where does the air come in? How can they all just grin and move their mouths when there's nothing left to breathe?

She stood alone, panicked in a crowd of unseeing eyes, chewing the side of her thumb.

A glass was shoved into her hand and a voice by her ear boomed out, "Don't know what you're drinking, lady, but you must need another one!"

Then, with the touch of the cold glass the dread was gone, and the faces turned into people, and she was one of them.

She turned to thank the man who had given her the drink,

but he was already shouldering away from her into the crowd. She saw only his white-shirted broad back and shining scalp. She sniffed at her glass, holding it up to look. Colorless, sweet-smelling, bubbles lining up to the surface. Gin and something, maybe. She drank, feeling the sharp warmth. Is it true about mixing your drinks being so bad? Oh well. Compete with Aaron on his own ground. She giggled aloud.

A blonde girl in red looked questioningly at her from beneath iridescent blue eyelids.

"My husband's taking care of drunks this year," Ellie explained. "I have to get in the act."

The girl gave her a puzzled smile and pushed on by.

George Kirkland rose up, a cheerful whale out of the human ocean. He clapped a big paw on Ellie's back. "Hey, great you could make it," he shouted. "Haven't seen your Johnny-boy yet, but I'll run into him. You get a baby-sitter for your drunk?"

"No, I just . . ." she began, but George was gone.

At the end of the living room where she stood twin stereo speakers quivered with sound, melodic sound, cream-rich with strings and sentiment. Between the speakers a fire danced in a broad brick fireplace. The rest of the long room was buried under the crush of people. She stood quietly by the fire sipping her drink, giving smile for smile with the faces that appeared and vanished near her.

Wilma, zigzagging through the room, jostled against her arm. "I've lost Byron!" she screamed above the music. "My sister's boy—you've met him, Ellie—have you seen him?"

"Not yet," Ellie said.

"Well, if you do . . . Oh, you have to have something to eat, dear . . . in the dining room, and have your drink filled, and if you do see Byron there're some folks I want him to meet . . ." Wilma worked her way on, still talking.

Something to eat. Ellie drained her glass and waded

through the crowd toward the dining room. The floor seemed far away as she stepped on it. The room was very warm. Was the gin that strong? But there had been the other drink at home. No, almost two drinks, really. Had she ever eaten dinner?

The dining room formed an L with the living room. The long table was a fragrant clutter of food. Turkey heaped in firm white slices on one platter; ham, pink and spicy, on another. A huge bowl of fondue, steaming over a squat candle. Plates of crackers in crazy quilt shapes. Mounds of celery and carrots and potato chips clustered around a bowl of fiery dip. Tiny pickles, crisp in melting ice. Fat hot chunks of garlic bread dripping butter into their wicker baskets.

The smells mingled in her nostrils. She was hungry. She took a paper plate from the stack at the end of the table and filled it, some of everything.

George Kirkland saw her and broke from a huddle of men. "What'll you have Ellie?" he asked. He took her glass. "You like bourbon and ginger ale, don't you?"

Ellie's mouth was full of turkey. She nodded. George disappeared into the kitchen, and then was back with the drink. Light tan this time, freshly bubbling.

"Thanks, George," she said.

She made her way over the distant floor to a spot by the fireplace. She leaned against the smoke-blackened brick, balancing her plate and glass, and watched the flames curl orange and red and blue around thick logs.

Wilma forged over, this time tugging her nephew in her wake. "I found Byron," she beamed. "Byron, you've met Ellie Clark. Wonderful boy, Ellie. Wonderful he could be here for our party!"

Byron grinned and winked. Ellie smiled at him peacefully.

"I can't find John, Ellie," Wilma complained. "He hasn't met Byron yet."

Ellie felt strangely comfortable, all her muscles loose. She looked at Wilma's frown. It was a funny frown. In such a red face, long, with big open pores dotting the long nose.

"Well, maybe he'll be at the table," Wilma decided. She was off again, pulling Byron after her.

Ellie slid down the brick at the side of the fireplace until she was sitting on the hearth rug. She put her plate down and took a long drink from her glass. Ginger ale fizzled in her nose. She ate a bit of garlic bread and drank again, holding the glass to her lips until it was empty.

Her lips felt swollen, enormous. She pressed them together. They tingled numbly. She touched the rim of the glass to her chin. That was numb, too. She never drank this much this fast. Three drinks in an evening, maybe two if they were strong. Well, no matter. Nothing matters very much.

She took a pickle from her plate. Her fingers felt the cold and knobby skin of it, but her fingers were not anything that belonged to her. They might be anybody's fingers. Interested, she watched her hand bring the pickle to her mouth.

Nothing was really part of her. Nothing was really her business. Not even her own hand. That's why nothing really matters, maybe.

She leaned back and for a moment was aware only of the pickle crunching between her teeth. Crisp, sharp, sour. Her mind was very clear. She felt good.

Nothing belongs to anyone, really. That's the point. Not even hands, or feet, or lips or hair. So maybe everything belongs to everybody. Yes, of course.

A few feet away, immensely high above her head, hands gestured. Hands with smooth fingers, white-polished nails, with a large ring, deep blue stone in twisted silver. She looked at the moving hands, then down at the small squarish hands that circled her glass. Which belonged? It didn't matter.

154

Everything was part of her. She was part of everything. There were no boundaries.

It was marvelously true.

"Can I get you another drink?"

She looked up. Byron Richardson. His tall figure stood over her in sharp outline against the blurred background of faces and hands and bodies. She gave him her empty glass.

"What are you drinking, Ellie?"

"You can get me . . . I had a gin and tonic once, I think. That was good."

Byron sniffed at the glass. "You must have had a regular chemistry set in here," he said.

She smiled and he grinned back at her. "Well, if you like chemistry sets," he said. "Be right back."

She leaned against the bricks again and closed her eyes. The world surged and ebbed around her with the pulse of her blood.

Then Byron was back carrying a glass for her and a glass for himself. "Sorry to be so long," he said, easing down onto the rug next to her. "I washed out your glass. Couldn't put the gin in on top of that chemistry set."

"Thanks," She took her glass and sipped from it.

Byron pushed the blond wave back from his forehead. "I've been trying to get to you, but Aunt Wilma's been having me meet everybody. I must have met the whole town at least twice by now. Only tonight I didn't exactly meet people, because every time we came up to anybody she'd just ask them if they'd seen someone else, and then we'd move on. Right now she's tearing up and down looking for a John Something."

Ellie giggled. "John. That's my husband." It was so funny.

"Your husband?" He stared at her sharply. Freckled skin crinkled below deep blue eyes. She looked into the eyes. What belongs to anyone?

"Your husband?" he repeated. "Aunt Wilma didn't say you were married."

Again she giggled. "Wilma never will find John," she said. "John's not here. I ran out on him. I'm not his type. His type is . . ." She giggled harder, seeing Aaron, his vacant eyes, his scrawny neck. She put her glass down on the hearth and laughed helplessly.

Byron watched her, trying to smile with her, puzzled.

"I'm not John's type," she said again, wiping her eyes from the laughter. "You married, Byron?"

"Me?" He looked startled. "Oh, I'm not married. Not nearly ready for all that business yet. Not for a long time." He ate a potato chip from Ellie's plate. "Actually I'm just out of dental school. This is my first year in practice. Lot of the men in my class got married while they were in school, but that's not for me. Little apartments, howling kids. Not for me. I'm not getting married until I can afford to do it right. Not fair to the woman, either, getting married before you can afford it."

He helped himself to another potato chip. He ate it, watching her thoughtfully. "Look, Ellie, really isn't your husband here?"

"My husband," Ellie echoed. "My husband really isn't here, Byron. My husband is much too busy to be here." She shrugged. "He probably hasn't even noticed I'm gone. It won't matter to him if I stay out all night. Isn't that nice?" She laughed again.

He laughed with her, showing even white teeth. Dentist's teeth. He hunched over closer to her on the hearth rug, rocking back and forth gently. "Some crowd," he said. "Bet almost everybody in town is here, really."

"I'll bet." She picked her drink up and swallowed deeply. She stared into the fireplace. A tiny blue flame bounced daintily from side to side under the bottom log. "Part of the fire, too," she murmured.

"What did you say?" he asked.

She swung away from the fire and looked at him. Blue eyes. Not pale. Wedgewood blue.

"I've been thinking," she told him. "We're all part of everything there is—that ever was. Everything that ever will be. All part of it and it's all part of us."

She sipped at her drink again, lifting her head, letting the warm liquid run down her throat. "Umm," she said. "Never thought about it before. That way. I mean, it's cells, you know—chromosomes—all that. Part of everybody who ever lived, back and back and back and back."

She looked dreamily into the fire. "Back before . . . part of the mud . . . water . . . sun . . ." She shook the ice around in her glass. "Part of the fire, part of . . ."

She leaned closer to the blue eyes. "I'm part of you, even," she told him.

She thought for a moment, drinking slowly. "Maybe that's what God is," she said. "If there is a God. Everything there is, all of us—maybe it's all God. Somebody said that once, I think. Can't remember who it was said that. But you know what I mean, don't you?

Byron scratched his hair, shaking the yellow wave back down over his forehead. "Well . . ." he said. He shifted a little on the rug. "I'm a Methodist, myself."

"Are you?" Ellie asked. "My mother used to be a Methodist. But when I was a child we went to the Presbyterian church. Their minister was better."

She looked around the shimmering room, at the people, vague, misty. Everything was rolling up and down, like a faulty television picture.

Cells and earth. Sun. God.

Beautiful.

Byron looked at his watch. He stood up. "Almost midnight, Ellie," he said.

As he said it the music stopped with a tooth-jarring scrape of the needle. George's voice boomed out strong over the houseful of voices. "Listen to me, everybody! Three minutes to midnight, ex-actly! Now get ready to do your damnedest!"

Wilma and two perspiring red-faced men shoved through the crowd carrying bushel baskets full of noisemakers. Clackers, whistles, horns, tinny kazoos.

Byron pulled Ellie to her feet. He dipped into the first basket to come near him and brought out a bright blue police whistle and a cone-shaped horn. He handed the horn to Ellie. It was covered with gaudy pictures of planets and space capsules.

George was standing on a chair now in the entrance to the dining room, waving his arm in wide arcs and shouting a countdown in the sudden silence: "Six . . . five . . . four . . . three . . . two . . . one . . . Happy New Year!"

The noise-makers exploded into sound; frenzied, screeching, clacking, howling, pounding on eardrums. Noise that swept them all with it through a small deafening eternity of din.

Ellie blew hard. Byron's whistle was loud in her ear. Then the whistling stopped and he pulled her to him. All around them couples were kissing, and his lips were on her lips, pressing hard. The Wedgewood eyes merged into one big eye just beyond her nose.

Then the blue divided and there were two eyes once more. Direct eyes with sparse, almost white lashes, in a face that smiled at her. It was a tidy face, somehow, square, freckled, smooth-skinned, the nose a little stubby. The blond hair had fallen forward again and coiled in tendrils on his forehead. He stood holding her lightly, and he smelled of soap and skin and some spicy shaving lotion. She shut her eyes to breathe

158

the smell and behind her closed lids her brain whirled. She took a step to balance herself, and felt his arm tighten around her, steadying her. She opened her eyes and rested against him. His body felt good touching hers. Solid. Male. She looked up at him again. A little taller than John. She leaned her head back to his shoulder. It fit in the soft place below the bone.

What would John think if he could see?

Well, John could have been here, if he'd wanted.

John has Aaron Sloane.

Once again she giggled.

Byron looked down at her. "What's the joke?" he asked.

"Oh, nothing." She peered into her glass. "Could I have another gin and tonic, do you think?"

"Come along," he said. He caught her free hand and pulled her after him, weaving around clumps of people, into the dining room. While he made the drinks the stereo music blared out again. Here and there couples were beginning to dance, crowded together, stepping in close little patterns.

George and Wilma were dancing near. George pumped Wilma's hand hugely up and down in time to the beat.

"Oh Ellie," Wilma called out. "I never could find John!" She pulled George to a stop and they swayed together in the same spot. "I guess I've just missed him so far."

"John isn't . . ." Ellie began, and dissolved helplessly in laughter as Wilma and George danced away.

Grinning and shaking his head, Byron handed her the filled glass. She drank slowly, still giggling now and then. Her body felt as if it were floating upright in warm bathwater.

She rubbed her hand on the rough wool of Byron's sleeve and looked at him. So tall. So blond, so certain.

And she was part of him, too, since back and back before the sun.

Beautiful.

She was happy. Everything was so easy, really. Living wasn't hard. All that made it hard was worrying about things. But if everybody was part of everything, what could there be to worry about?

In a far-off corner of her mind a thin thread of words spun out: You've had too much to drink.

"Nonsense," she murmured. "What does it matter?"

"What did you say?" Byron asked, bending his head to hers.

She smiled at him, not knowing what he meant. Not really caring what he meant. Her eyelids were hot.

"It's hot in here," she told him.

He said something and seemed to wait for an answer, but the words he said were lost in the tide of sound around them. She nodded, and felt herself sway a little, and reached for his hand. He pulled her through the crowd and she followed him, walking through air as thick as water, smiling here and there into friendly eyes.

Then they were in the little room off the hall where coats were piled and he was sliding the fleecy red jacket over her arms. And then she was easing her feet into the white boots.

And then they were in the cold, snow-smelling night, under a sky jumping with haloed stars.

He held out a hand, testing the air. "Stopped snowing," he said. With an arm around her shoulders, he helped her to his car—a white marshmallow in the line of fat white marshmallows that rimmed the curb. He scooped snow from the windshield with his arm. It was cold and dry; it fell off easily, leaving the glass clear,

"Car'll go all right," he said confidently. "It's a good little car. VW—one of the new ones. Put the chains on it this afternoon."

160

He opened the door and helped her in. Relaxed, unquestioning, she leaned back in her seat. She looked out the window at white on black, black on white. He slid into the driver's seat and started the motor. The little car pulled neatly away from the curb, shaking off snow. Smooth snow and darkness floated past the windows, close, friendly. A safe, small world.

Byron glanced over at the green slacks below Ellie's jacket. "You're dressed for the weather," he commented.

"Just didn't ever change," she said. She looked at his profile. Square. Everything about it square. And . . . clean was the right word. Like a Boy Scout.

But John was the Boy Scout. Good deeds. Aaron— sick . . . scrawny . . . stray . . . "Byron," she asked suddenly, "Do you ever take in stray cats?"

"Stray cats?" He laughed. "Oh sure, when I was a kid I used to. Doesn't everybody? I'd drag them home all the time—tell my mom they just followed me. But I got over it. I grew up." He shot a glance at her. "Why do you want to know?"

"I just wondered."

"Had a big German shepherd when I was a kid. Meanest fellow ever was. But was I crazy about him! I called him Butch . . ."

She watched the line of tree trunks shift beyond the window as he swung the steering wheel to the right. Ahead of them the road shone in the headlights, white, unmarked, hardly to be told from the wide span of ground on either side. Edison Park. In the snow. Beautiful.

She sighed happily. "Beautiful," she said. The word was hard to say. Her tongue felt too large.

She pulled off a mitten and laid her hand on the window glass beside her. She looked at the hand, darker than the snow, lighter than the night. She spread her fingers apart and saw snow and night between them. She looked and the snow drew nearer than her hand, her hand seemed to drift out into the night. "Beautiful," she said again, carefully.

The little car cut its solitary trail through the park. Chains ground the snow with a muted jangle.

Byron swerved to the curb that was just a rise in the snow, and stopped the car.

"Want to get out?" he asked.

She nodded.

He climbed out and held the door for her. She stood up and sank into snow that reached her boot-tops. The car was parked by the little duck pond. No ducks there now. Just a kidney-shaped field of snow, rounded with bushes that bent under their white cushions. She found Byron's hand and together they tramped to the edge of the pond.

"It's frozen hard under the snow," Byron said. "There were some kids skating here yesterday."

He pulled her on. When her feet left the ground and stood over snow-covered ice she could not tell the difference. Hand in hand the two of them shuffled to the middle of the pond. The world was a kind, small room around them. A circle of snow below, a circle of stars close overhead. Silent, all the night-noises drowned in the muffling snow.

She thrust out her arms to hold it all, and started to fall. She caught at Byron. He held her closely. She turned her face to him and again he kissed her, harder this time, longer. She felt the even teeth under his lips.

When his face moved back she snuggled her head under his shoulder as she had before.

He needed to understand about being part of everything. Tell him. Tell him.

The thoughts shot swift and clear through her mind, but the words to say them hovered in a tangle. Sorting out the words was too much work. Instead she leaned closer against

162

him. The night touched her face coldly, but inside her skin she was warm. So very warm.

They went back to the car and he helped her in. He drove slowly along the winding roads of the park. He talked and she listened. Not to his words. To the sound of his voice. She shut her eyes and could see his voice. Deep voice. Brown, like polished wood, glowing.

He asked a question, and asked it again. She opened her eyes and pulled her mind into itself to understand the words.

"I asked you if you wanted to come in for a drink," he said. "This is where I'm staying."

She sat up and peered out the window. They had left the park. The car was stopped in front of a huge orange sign that blasted on and off in her eyes, blinding her to the snow.

"You're staying here?" she asked. She blinked at the neon. The sharp-orange tubes twisted out the words MOTEL. VACANCY.

Something wrong about going in. She rubbed her face, trying to understand.

"It's a good motel," Byron was saying.

Motel. Tiny words, marching in a line at the back of her brain: Don't go in.

Why not? John. John wouldn't like it.

She shut her eyes once more. John's face. John's eyes— worried. Looking, tender, worried, all-absorbed, into blank watery eyes—dead eyes—Aaron Sloane's eyes.

The two pairs of eyes vanished in a burst of red. "I'd like to come in for a drink," she said clearly.

Don't go in.

Well, what if I do go in? It's nothing but words.

Behind her eyelids she stared at the line of little words and watched them march on, and on, and out of her brain.

FOURTEEN

IT WAS TOO HOT. COVERS LAY DAMP AND HEAVY ON ELLIE'S BACK.
She jerked them down to her waist. She drew herself together
like an inchworm, dug the top of her head into the pillow,
stretched flat again. Drove her body into the mattress as if
the vanishing dream were there.

The mattress quivered under her. Her skin felt the too-
warm air, the slippery sheet. The dream was sinking out of
reach.

What was the dream? She had to remember. It was the
answer to everything, somehow, to all the questions.

Without opening her eyes she turned on her side and
nestled her back to the man beside her. His thigh, naked,
touched hers. He moved closer. She rested her hand on his
leg.

The dream. The answer.

She opened her eyes and blinked with the sudden light.

The light filtered between white slats, through strawberry-
red draperies.

She lifted her head.

A cream painted radiator snuffled steadily beside a blonde
wood bureau. Across from her sat a blonde-armed easy chair—

164

her slacks, her brown sweater crumpled on its red cushion. A brassiere strap twisted from under the sweater.

She sat up. Her hands jumped to her naked breasts In the room's heat her hands on them were as cold as stones in winter.

Pain slapped from side to side in her head.

Oh God no.

She gathered the sheet to her and looked down at the bed.

Byron Richardson lay on his side, his legs drawn up loosely. The squared-off jaw hung slack, the white dentist's teeth showed. Beneath his sleeping eyes the fringe of sparse white lashes rested peacefully on high cheekbones. The blond hair had pasted itself in spring-coils to his damp forehead. The strawberry-red bedspread lay around his hips, rose and fell smoothly over his trim stomach. An arm, freckled at the shoulder, was flung upward. The broad fist bunched the pillow under his head.

"Oh dear God." She shaped the words soundlessly with her lips. She pulled up her knees and laid her throbbing head on them. Nausea clenched her.

It's not real. I'm not like that. It has to be that I'm not like that.

She pressed her head to her sharp knees, fighting back the nausea, fighting back the night. But the night had happened.

I didn't know what was going on. I had so much to drink—I was too mixed up. I can't even remember . . .

But she did remember. Everything there was to remember. The drinks. The motel glasses were wrapped in waxed paper "for your protection." Byron had made some joke about that, peeling it off.

Drinking beside Byron on the strawberry-red spread, moving her head to set the room in motion, to see it swirl, laughing . . .

Once there had been something she wanted to explain to Byron, but explaining seemed too much trouble.

She'd talked about John.

No, I musn't remember that.

In the morning's hard light she dropped back on the mattress, twisting her face into the pillow. God, the things she'd said about John. Terrible things. Things she could never have meant.

I didn't say them. How can I make it be that I didn't say them? She pressed her hands to her eyes, wrinkled her forehead tight.

It all happened. You can't make it be different now. So remember, remember all of it, remember it like a penance.

Remember Byron's lips, hard, almost hurting; the sweet bourbon taste of his tongue. Square hands, taking your glass, moving on your skin, unhooking your brassiere, touching, stroking under the brown sweater. Remember clinging to him, swimming with the room. Laughing. Always laughing.

There had been a reason why it was all right, all fair. It hadn't mattered then that she couldn't remember the reason—it was there, just beyond the laughing.

Remember being naked, raw-naked, touching his nakedness. The two of you holding each other, moving together on the bedspread, under the bedspread, on the slippery sheet. Remember the way his body felt—like John's and yet so strangely not like John's.

Behind her eyelids John's face had been a red and hateful burst of fire. Her body had strained with fire.

Remember your wanting, the hot red wanting, made of the fire. Remember his back under your digging fingers, clutching him furiously, the pair of you a bright center for the skyrocket-popping world.

Remember pulling him tight, crying to him oh faster, harder—

166

Something black behind me, blackness coming up behind me—quick before it catches up, before it's all too late.

But it could not be quick enough. The lurking blackness caught you and took you and deluged you, uncompleted. There was nothing left but blackness.

Chill. Remember how you shivered and could not stop shivering, feeling it be finished for him.

He lay beside you and held you. He kissed your throat. He thought it was finished for you, too. He thought it was all right. But it was not all right. John is my husband and it was not all right. Something was supposed to have made it all right, but I can't remember what.

He had slept after that, and she had turned to her side and cried tightly, her hand over her mouth for silence. After a while she had slept too.

That was last night. Remember it. It happened.

Now, in the morning, in the too-warm room, she made herself sit up once more. She huddled on the edge of the bed. The gurgle and hiss of the radiator assaulted her. Her stomach surged. She got up, and without straightening, she groped her way into the tiny white bathroom. She threw the door shut behind her, knelt on a white paper bathmat before a spotless white toilet and vomited convulsively, again and again.

At last she reached for the edge of the washbowl and pulled herself up. She leaned over the bowl's cold rim, resting her forehead on the mirror.

Then she straightened and looked into the mirror. A caricature stared back. Brown hair stringing down, stiff with hairspray, separating around the ears. Bare shoulders, bones under skin, knobs and hollows. Colorless lips, lines of dried lipstick clinging in their creases. Nose a pink blotch against drained cheeks. Big eyes, all pupil, grotesque with smeared mascara. Eyes that could almost be Aaron Sloane's eyes.

She looked at the unknown face and a word began in her mind, kept thrashing there, would not leave. An old-fashioned word—one you don't use any more. A pitiless word. Adultery.

It means last night, it means me. Here, down in this blackness, what am I?

She looked away from the mirrored caricature. She turned the water on, bent and held her mouth under the stream of it, rinsed away the worst of the sourness. For a moment she leaned against the door, then she pulled it open and walked slowly back into the bedroom.

Byron lay on his back, watching her, smiling. She looked down at her naked body.

Well, what difference does it make, any more? He's seen it all.

She dropped onto the edge of the bed. He reached out and cupped his hand over one of her breasts, worked the nipple between his fingers gently, askingly. He pulled her close.

He's going to do it again. Well, that doesn't matter either. It's too late to matter now. She lay back and let her eyes fall shut.

His face pressed on hers, hot-smelling. His tongue felt her mouth. His fingers touched her nipple, pulling it gently, his other hand stroked her stomach, her legs, her thighs. She lay still, hardly aware.

"Ellie," he urged. "Ellie." His breath was damp on her cheek. She opened her eyes. He was frowning at her, the light hair tangled to his eyebrows. Sweat stood out on his lip.

She turned half toward him and let her arm fall over his shoulder. It's not his fault.

Can't it be his fault, some way?

But the clear and traitorous remembering kept the night what it had been. It had not been his fault. He had wanted her, yes, but she had led the way.

168

Her words came back to her, unforgotten: I'm not John's type . . . I ran out on him . . . won't matter to him if I stay out all night . . . I'd like to come in . . . won't matter if I ,stay . . . I ran out on him . . . if I stay out all night . . .

Other things—the way she had met his New Year's kiss, the way she had leaned against him . . . It wasn't his fault.

Aaron Sloane, how much do you have to drink before you can't remember?

"Ellie?" His voice sounded scratchy. His cheek was scratchy, like John's in the morning.

She turned to him and found his mouth with hers. She stroked his back. It's not his fault, no need to make him pay. None of it matters anyway, now.

She touched her tongue to his earlobe. Salty. She felt, without caring, his hands on her. Before last night, there had never been anyone but John.

She felt the throbbing in her head, her ears, her eyes. There was nothing in her to give him now, but her body could pretend to give.

If I don't have to feel. I'm too tired to have to feel, there's too much blackness. Please, no feeling.

She did the things she knew he wanted, and wondered, moving her hollow body with his body, that there should be so little she really had to feel.

His head pulled away and his fingers tightened on her back. She watched his contorted, undefended face, and she knew a loneliness more complete than all her terrors of aloneness.

He lay relaxed, holding her beside him, keeping her head in the warmth of his chin and shoulder, stroking her hair. "Good, Ellie?" he asked.

"Good," she lied.

He grinned. "You're really something, you know."

She shut her eyes, locked in blackness. Pain sliced a line

down her face and split through her eyeballs. Nausea pulsed in her stomach.

His voice came to her from far away beyond the pain. "Ellie, just what is it with your husband?" he asked.

"John?"

"That his name? What is it with you and him, anyway?"

"John." She twisted out of his arms and sat on the edge of the bed. Her stomach lurched. She bent double, her hands clammy around her ankles, her forehead burning on her knees, and let the sickness subside. She wanted to be home. More than anything she had ever wanted in her life.

"Byron," she whispered, "please take me home."

He sat up, surprised. "You mean now?"

"Yes. Now. For God's sake, right now."

The red Volkswagon whirred on its chains over hard-packed snow. Sun glared on the snow, sparking to fire a million diamond-flecks. The sky was cloudless, a shining blue that arched above the white. From somewhere came the steady growl of a bulldozer, clearing a trail for the thin traffic of New Year's morning. Ellie crouched in her seat, aware of nothing but the cutting pain and the nausea that welled through her body.

"Don't have any hangover, myself," Byron said. "Guess you were drinking more than I was. Well, it's too bad."

He looked at her quickly and then quickly back at the road. "Ellie, you are sure about what you said—that you could take care of things all right? If your husband wants to know where you've been all night?"

"Oh. Yes. I'll tell him . . . something." She rubbed her swollen eyes. "You don't have to worry about that, Byron."

She wondered, through the pain, what she could possibly say to John, and then knew that there was nothing she could say at all. She couldn't lie to him. She was too tired. Everything hurt too much.

John . . . John . . . the blackness is real.

Byron's gloved finger traced the line of her chin. She lifted her head. Behind her eyes the hammer-pulse beat harder.

"Hey, I have to get back to Chicago today," he said. "But I'll be in town again. Soon, maybe, if I can work it. We can get together next time I'm here, you think?"

She looked at him dully. The words he said dropped vacantly into her mind among the hammer blows. She didn't answer them.

The car swung around a curve between heaped drifts. She squinted through her window into the brightness. "Here's your aunt's house," she said. "I think I'd better walk from here."

"Well . . ." he bent to study her face. "Are you up to walking?"

"Yes." She swallowed to keep down the sickness. "I can walk. I think it would be better that way."

"Well, you know best."

She sat motionless while he stopped the car. His kiss was snow-cold on her closed lips. "Ellie, remember, I'll be in touch with you," he said.

"Goodbye," she answered.

She ducked to climb out of the car, made herself stand straight and wave as he drove off. Then she moved over the deep hidden walks toward home.

Home. John's home. Keith's, Betsy's. Oh God, why?

At the corner of the drive she stopped still in front of the bittersweet vine, snow coated, massed on its fence. The clustered berries burned through the snow, a thousand shouting orange flames. She looked at them and the tears that waited in her throat swelled up and burst out. She folded into the soft snow, not feeling its cold, rocking back and forward by the vine.

"Damn you!" she sobbed to it. "I hate you! Why won't your berries fall off? Why do you have to be beautiful?"

Hands and straggled hair covering her face, she sat in the snow and cried.

Then she pushed herself up, touched the nearest flaming cluster softly, and crossed through dense and heaving blackness to the house.

FIFTEEN

SHE HAD NO WORDS READY FOR SAYING WHEN SHE CLOSED THE
door behind her. She stood in the darkened living room,
blinking and widening snow-dazed eyes. Waiting for it to
happen, whatever would happen.

Nothing happened.

The house kept still.

Slowly, wondering, she walked into the kitchen, switched
on the light, looked around her. Cups holding skinned-over
dregs of coffee. Ashtrays heaped from a long night of smoking—cigar butts, squashed ends of cigarettes, crumbling dol-
lops from a pipe. Spilled tobacco freckling the green table
top. A necktie, still tied, dropped beside a nearly empty bourbon bottle. John's glasses lying on a damp dishtowel.

She looked at her watch, squinting to keep its hands from
jumping as she tried to read them. Past nine. Wasn't anyone up? Aaron?

She went down the hall. The door to Keith's room stood
open. She looked in, letting the door-frame prop her. Aaron
was there in Keith's bed—a mound of twisted covers sprout-
ing at the top a spikey cluster of hair.

John's easy chair had been pulled into the room; someone sprawled in it, covered with a blanket. John?

She took a step nearer.

John. John sleeping, his head thrown back, his face colorless in the light that crept in around drawn shades. He looked exhausted. The line between his tangled eyebrows was a deep cleft. Sleep had not loosened the tenseness of his lips. The short dark hair stood up in clumps from his forehead.

She looked at him and the pain hit sharp in her head and lungs and stomach.

She turned away and climbed through pain to their own bedroom. As she went by she looked through Betsy's door. Whit was asleep on the cot by Betsy's empty bed.

The children?

Well, someone would be taking care of them. Grace would have them, of course.

Taking better care of them than I did, last night.

She reached the bed and fell on it, lay as she fell, doubled on top of the spread.

She was home.

And no talking needed, yet. No thinking needed, yet. Just home.

She kicked off her loafers and squirmed in under the blankets. She pulled them tight over her bursting head until the room and the world were gone in a darkness more kind than the darkness inside her. She folded up like an unborn baby and went to sleep.

She slept for a long time. Now and then she would wake to the pain and a room that whirled sickeningly; then she would go down into sleep once more. Sometimes, when she woke, there were people. Grace's face, bright lips puckered with concern, floating above her. Whit, looking in.

Once, she thought, Aaron Sloane's stooped figure loomed in the doorway.

174

And John. John's voice, insistent. "Ellie, are you sick or something? What in heaven's name is the matter with you?" She shrank into herself. His hand was heavy on her shoulder.

Not yet. Please, not yet. I'm not ready.

"John. I . . . guess it's a virus or something. I was coming down with it at the party." It was hard to talk. "I'm . . . John, please, just let me rest a while longer."

Whirlpooling again into sleep.

"Could you manage some soup?" Grace's voice, soothing. "Can you sit up, Ellie?"

Grace's hand, cool on the back of her neck. Being kind. Why do they have to be kind?

"Grace, you have the children?"

"Of course. Don't you worry about them one little bit. I took them home with me last night, just in case there was—oh you know—any trouble with Aaron. Whit's staying with them while I'm over here. Now try this."

Ellie let the firm hand guide her to a sitting position. A soup bowl steamed on the bedside table. She leaned over and looked into it. Noodles and chunks of meat and vegetables swimming in a pale broth. The steam invaded her nostrils, beefy, herb-smelling, mingled with Grace's flowery perfume.

Her stomach convulsed.

"I just can't, Grace."

She slid back down in the bed. The pillow felt damp under her cheek.

Grace clapped a practiced hand to her forehead. "You don't seem to have any fever," she said. "But I don't know what all's going around. Maybe we'd better call a doctor. John was asking me what I thought about it."

Ellie's eyes jolted open. "Oh no," she said, alarmed. "No doctor. Please. I'm not sick. I mean, I don't need a doctor."

She pulled herself up on an elbow, then dropped down again, fighting the nausea. "I went to that party, you know. I don't know why I wanted to go. I wish I hadn't gone. But I've got a . . . I had a lot more to drink than I usually have. That's all. That's really all that's wrong with me, Grace."

"Well, Ellie Clark!" Grace laughed richly. "I never thought I'd see you, of all people, with a hangover! Anyway, I'm glad it isn't the flu or something."

She smoothed Ellie's covers and stood looking at her thoughtfully with a hand propping her chin.

"Now let me think what's good for it," she said. "Whit still talks about the terrible hangovers he used to have. Before we were married, you know, when he was drinking so much." Grace shook her head. The sculptured hair quivered. "That must have been an awful time. Poor, poor man. "

Then unexpectedly she laughed again. "We could ask Aaron what he takes for a hangover. He's the real expert."

Ellie winced. "Is Aaron still here?" she asked. "I thought I saw him. I wasn't quite sure."

"Aaron's still very much here," Grace said grimly. "Trying his best to get us to keep him here, too. Oh, John and Whit haven't weakened yet. But John didn't want to leave with Aaron until he knew what was happening with you. He'll be glad to know it's nothing but too much party. Now you just lie still, and I'll see what I can find for your hangover." Grace whisked out of the bedroom.

Ellie closed her eyes, her body spinning. Too much party.

Round and round behind dark eyelids. Is there medicine to change what happened, Grace? Bring it, quickly, bring it.

Grace was back, pushing her up again in the bed.

"Paragoric," Grace was saying, pouring liquid into a spoon from a small brown bottle. "I found some in your medicine cabinet and I called Whit, and he said it was about as good as anything. Now here."

She tipped the spoon into Ellie's mouth. Ellie lay back. The liquid burned its way cleanly down her throat.

Grace capped up the bottle and sat on the edge of the bed. "Ellie, you know those men sat up most of the night with Aaron," she said. "Measuring out doses of whiskey every couple of hours. They were half dead. Aaron wasn't too much trouble, though, or at least not as much trouble as they thought he might be. I went home with the children just a little bit after you left."

"I'm sorry," Ellie murmured. "The children . . ."

"Now, none of that, Ellie Clark." Grace's lips pursed. "You know I love to have them. And with all of us around there wasn't any reason why you shouldn't have gone to the Kirkland's party. But you really didn't need that much to drink."

She laughed. "I guess you'll know that, next time. Anyway, Aaron did his usual talking last night, Whit said. More of that business about not being able to stand the lock-up, and how he didn't know what he'd do if he had to go there, and so on and so forth. But the men didn't give in. And apparently Aaron didn't do anything much except talk. Whit said he and John got to sleep about five in the morning. Aaron seemed a lot calmer by then—he wasn't waking up any more. He slept until just an hour or two ago."

She looked at the tiny jeweled watch embedded in her wrist. "Past noon now. They'll have to be taking that man away soon if they're ever going to."

She stood up, puffing a bit. "You'll be all right now, won't you?"

Ellie nodded. She watched Grace bustle out of the room.

The nausea was letting up some. The paragoric must be helping.

As the sickness dulled, the other pain—the remembering—grew sharper. Swelled monstrously, until she didn't know how to stand it. For the hundredth time she drove the memory through her aching brain—all of it, from the time she left for the party to the moment when Byron had let her out of his car this morning. The remembering hurt—she needed it to hurt.

Everybody was being so kind.

I can't stand having them be kind. If only they would hate me. Why don't I tell them? They'd hate me then. I don't want that. But kindness is worse, when I know I'm not what they think. I could stand their hate.

But John.

She twisted on the bed. No. Not John. I can't live without John.

Then you'll live with John, she thought, and he'll never hate you, because he'll never know what you did to him. He'll never know what you are and he'll always love you, Ellie Clark, can you stand that?

No.

No, no. Desperation drove her up from the bed. Her cold feet reached for the floor. "John!" she called. "John, please!"

She stood by the bed, holding on to the headboard for steadiness, ready for his hate. Needing it the way one needs food, or water when there is no water. Or sleep.

"John!"

He has to know. Now, he has to hate me, now, so it can all be over.

"You call, Ellie?" John's voice from the living room sounded curt. "Save it, will you? I can't come right now."

"Hurry, John," she said, but not loudly enough for him to hear her. Her legs felt boneless. She slid down the side of the bed and sat on the floor. She let her head lie back against the mattress.

Footsteps to the door. Now.

"Ellie?"

Grace. Not John. "Come on now, Ellie. There isn't a

thing you have to get up for. Go back to bed and tell me what it is you want."

"John. Please tell John I have to see him."

Grace, a disapproving hen. "John's having a talk with Aaron. He can't come right now."

Grace, helping her into bed, straightening the covers. "Would you like some ice or something?"

"Just John." Why won't she understand I can't wait?

Grace plunked down heavily on the mattress.

"Well, Ellie, the fact is Aaron's giving John a good deal of trouble right now," she said. "When he first woke up this morning he was completely resigned to going to the mental hospital. Or said he was. He told John and Whit he'd been thinking it all over, that he could stand the lock-up if they could cure him there. He said he really couldn't go on the way he had been—that he did want to get well. He said he guessed there wasn't any other way he could do it."

Grace settled the covers more firmly over Ellie's shoulders.

"So that seemed all right," she went on. "We were all pretty relieved, you can just imagine. Then a little while ago he started pacing around the house as shaky as he ever was, saying he can't take the lock-up unless he gets a few hours by himself first. Downtown, by himself. Well, you've heard that one, Ellie." She sighed deeply.

Why won't she bring John? Why does she just keep talking?

"He's arguing and carrying on the way he did before," Grace said. "He wants John to let him off downtown and pick him up early in the evening. Promises he'll be ready and waiting. I can tell how much that means."

"I see." Ellie turned to her side.

So she couldn't even tell John about last night. She couldn't even make him hate her. Aaron Sloane could spoil that, too.

Grace smoothed the hair back from her forehead and got up. "Now why don't you try to get a little more sleep?" she suggested. "You'll feel better soon. These things don't last forever."

Alone, Ellie stared at the closed door. They can last forever, she thought. Longer.

But people do what you did all the time, Ellie Clark—it doesn't matter to them.

It matters to me. It will matter to John. God, it will matter to John.

She forced her mind on, beyond the time when John would know, and hate. Nothing there—just emptiness. But time is never empty, really. Things go on—you eat, sleep, work. Even when it doesn't matter any more, things go on. What will be happening after John knows?

She sat up again, sharply.

The children. What will happen to them? Things may be ruined for me, past mending. If I destroy all that's left with John . . . what about the children? She lay back, making herself think.

If John doesn't find out about last night . . . Could I let him not find out?

If he doesn't find out, then, for the children, nothing will be changed.

Could I stand it that way? Can I stand it either way?

With a sudden violence she threw her face into the pillow. No. Not either way. Boxed in, caught, no way out—why? In the name of God, why?

Finally she slept again, and her dreams were disconnected fragments, tumbling bits and pieces of some great dark shattered thing.

At last she gave them up, and came awake. She got out of bed and walked slowly, not quite so dizzy now, to the closet. She stood before the open closet door and pulled the brown sweater off over her head. She brushed the hair from her eyes and undid her brassiere, dropping it on the floor. Then she stripped off the wrinkled slacks, and her underpants. She bunched all the clothes together and stuffed them into the laundry hamper.

She stood still, keeping herself steady. Naked. Empty. Down to nothing.

Nothing.

Then she took her bathrobe from its hook, put it on, and tied it around her waist. What to say, what not to say, what to be—she didn't know. Or how to be, or why. She opened the bedroom door and walked out into the hall.

John was just coming out of Keith's room. The overcoat Aaron had been using was draped over his arm. His eyes looked worried, the thick eyebrows were out of all order.

Suddenly she wanted to run to him, to cry out for him to take care of her, as he had always taken care of her. There hadn't been anything John couldn't make all right.

Until now. He couldn't make this all right.

He glanced at her briefly as he hurried to the living room. He didn't seem aware of her. Slowly she followed behind him. She sat on a straight-backed chair near the door to the hall.

Aaron was standing in front of the couch. His back was turned to Ellie. He was staring through the picture window. His hand shook as it jerked a cigarette mechanically in and out of his mouth.

Grace wasn't there. Home, probably, with Whit, taking care of Keith and Betsy.

John touched Aaron on the arm. "Here's your coat," he said.

Aaron threw down his cigarette. He smashed it into the rug with his shoe and spun around. "You have to give me some time first, Mr. Clark," he said. His voice was hoarse. "I told you I can't stand it unless I have some time to myself first. Going right in there with all those crazy people."

"We've talked about it all we're going to, Aaron," John said evenly. "You agreed. We let you spend the night here because you agreed to enter the hospital today. That's all there is to it. Now here's your coat. I'm ready to go."

A look that could only be hatred sparked in Aaron's watery eyes. "I'll go to the hospital," he said. "I told you I would. I'll be ready when you come to pick me up. Just a few hours by myself first—that's not much."

"No," John said. His voice kept steady, but the hand that held the overcoat dropped a little lower.

Aaron lit another cigarette and tossed the match into the ashtray. Behind the smoke his eyes narrowed. "A few hours," he said again. "You have to let me, Mr. Clark. You can't make a prisoner out of me."

He dragged on the cigarette, watching John through the thin lines of eyes, then he ground it out and lit another. He dropped that one, glowing, into the ashtray. He covered his eyes with both hands, the fingers bent into claws.

"I'm no prisoner," he muttered. He walked out of the living room. The door to Keith's bedroom slammed shut.

John started after him, then stopped. He looked down at the coat over his arm. He fingered its lapel.

"I half want to turn him loose," he said. "Just let him off on a street corner someplace and forget him."

"Can you just forget him?" Ellie asked.

He looked up, startled, as if he hadn't known she was there, as if he'd been talking to himself. The line deepened between his eyes. "If he doesn't meet me, that will have to be the end of it," he said.

"You know he won't meet you. And you know he'll call sometime. Can you still let it be the end, even if he calls?"

He stared at her. "Ellie, I think Aaron Sloane is my problem," he said sharply. "He was my problem last night when you went chasing off to that idiot party and got yourself plastered. Last night you didn't give a good goddamn what I did with him."

Ellie jumped from her chair. Without any warning at all the emptiness in her filled with fury. Like the fury of last night, the fury that sent her off to the party, to Byron Richardson.

"Maybe you had another problem besides Aaron Sloane last night!" she shot out. "Because I did more than get plastered last night, John. Let me tell you what else I did. I spent the night with a man. At his motel. A man who thinks I'm a lot more interesting than some old drunk!"

She was crying. Viciously she scrubbed at the tears. "Now let that be your problem, John Clark!"

John's hands tightened on the coat he held. "Ellie," he said. "Don't play games with me."

"It's no game!" Her voice was shrill, the words strung together. "He's a dentist from Chicago, and he was at the party. And he's nice. We left the party and went to his motel and I spent the night with him, and I felt awful about it today but now I'm glad I did it, because you don't care about me at all, just about that shitty old drunk in there. And you won't forget about him, no matter what you say!"

John's arms hung at his sides. The coat flapped loose. "Did you . . ." he tried. "You didn't . . ."

"Yes we did! Twice!" She was shouting. She pulled her voice down. "Once last night when I was drunk and once this morning when I was cold, cold sober. And he said I was really something!"

She broke away from his eyes, from anything he might have said, ran back to bed frantically. For a meaningless time she heard nothing but her own gulping sobs.

Then there was the muffled sound of the doorbell. Whit's

voice in the hall. John, answering him, too low, too controlled. A drawn-out muttering from Aaron.

Then a creaking tattoo of feet and the closing of the front door, like the period at the end of a sentence.

The empty house lay quiet.

SIXTEEN

IT WAS LATE BEFORE JOHN CAME BACK. THE AFTERNOON DROPPED insignificantly into night. Not hurting any more, not angry or afraid or even thinking any more, Ellie had spent the hours wandering numbly through the rooms, sitting on the couch, at the bare kitchen table, staring out through blank windows.

Once a boy came to the door carrying a shovel. He wanted to clear the snow from the driveway. Ellie had looked beyond him at the single set of tire tracks leading away from the house. "No, I don't think we'll need it cleared," she had told him.

Near evening Grace called, offering to keep the children on for dinner and the night.

"They've been so good, Ellie—they've been having a fine time. We're taking down the Christmas tree. Keith unhooked all the lights and put them away, and Betsy is in there now packing ornaments. She's so careful putting them in the box— you should see her. Do let them stay!"

"Yes, that's fine," Ellie had said dully. Then, with an effort, "It's kind of you, Grace, Thanks."

She was in bed when John's tires crunched through the snow at last, when he bumped open the kitchen door.

He came into the bedroom. She lay still, looking at his

closed face. His eyes kept carefully away from hers. "I let Aaron off at the corner of Edwards and Main," he said. His voice was almost a monotone. "I went back a while ago, but he wasn't there."

Silently he changed to his pajamas and got into bed. He lay far from her, turned away from her. For all she knew, he might have gone to sleep.

She looked at his back, unmoving beneath the blankets. She wanted to talk, to tell him . . . John. John, what could I tell you? Anger, fear, longing, all shouting to be said and done away with. There was no way to say them.

Beat against his silence, batter the tight door of it—you locked that door yourself, Ellie Clark, you can't say a word to him now. You can't even reach out and touch him with your hand.

There were so many things he could have said. He didn't say them. He only turned away and left her helpless.

But did you earn anything to say, Ellie Clark? Last night?

Between the two of them sat the thing that divided them. Last night, dividing them.

Or something more than last night? Nights, days of not being whatever—who knows whatever?—we might have been to each other? Or why would last night have happened?

But what might they have been, and for how long had they not been that? For only since Aaron Sloane? She lay awake, asking, having no answers, finding nothing ever to say.

Days followed days and the thing between them grew in silence. They never spoke of it. They lived together in the same house, they slept together in the same bed, but never touching, careful not to touch, apart.

Over her typewriter or standing at the sink above forgotten dishwater, Ellie thought what they might say to each other. She lived through daydreams. Some ended with John storming out, away from her, as she had stormed out that night. In some she was the one who left, bringing the children with her or leaving them to him. Sometimes she imagined talking with John, the two of them just talking and talking, hours of talking, until everything that had happened was gone, drowned under words, and they loved each other as they used to do. Or perhaps as they had never really done. How do people need to love each other?

The daydreams all ended with something happening. Anything at all that happened, no matter what, would be better than these sealed-off days through which they moved.

She tried, sometimes, to call back the anger that had sent her off that night. Could such anger have been part of her? She wondered, unbelieving. All feeling was drained from her now, leaving nothing in its place.

Once in a while she would see John's eyes watching her thoughtfully, over the table, from a doorway, across a room, and her hand would be shaking, and she would find herself waiting to hear what he never said.

Sometimes she would be ready to go to him, to do anything to crack their silence open. But then, always, she would turn away. Sometimes she thought she might leave him, just pack and go while he was at work. But she couldn't do that, either.

Something in their silence paralyzed her. Seemed to paralyze them both, more and more the longer it went on.

One night, late, when John was asleep beside her, she got out of bed and went into the bathroom. She opened the medicine cabinet, seeing her stark white face swing away in the mirror on its door.

Pushed far back on the top shelf there was a bottle of phenobarbital tablets, an old prescription of John's. She took the bottle down. It was nearly full. John had never liked to use pills much.

She held the bottle in both hands, looking at it. Then she twisted off the cap and poured the pills out in her hand, all of them. Awkwardly, with her other hand, she took her glass from the toothbrush holder and filled it with water.

For a time that had no measurement she stood barefoot on the cold tile floor, the glass of water in one hand and the white mound of pills in the other. Paralyzed.

At last she poured the water down the washbowl drain. She fed the pills, one by one, back into their bottle. She replaced the cap, and set the bottle on the top shelf once more. Then she sat on the edge of the bathtub and cried.

When she had cried herself empty she got into bed again. She lay on her back and stared quietly at the light fixture—it was a pale square against the dark square of the ceiling, and she stared at it because it had no meaning at all. She wasn't able to live. It was the final failure that she wasn't even able to die.

When she had watched it long enough, the dark square faded and day came. And led into another day, more days.

They heard nothing from Aaron Sloane. When Grace talked wonderingly, almost triumphantly, about his staying away, Ellie felt distantly grateful that he had. At least there wasn't Aaron, too.

But many times, in bed at night, Betsy and Keith asked for Aaron. If only in that way, he was still with them.

One afternoon Byron Richardson called. Ellie listened, unbelieving, to the half-familiar voice on the phone.

"I'll just be in town for the day, Ellie—I thought if you could get away . . ."The voice went on, warm, easy, from a place without silence. A place where pain was not needed. A place much farther than Chicago.

". . . this restaurant that just opened up on the edge of town—steaks are real good . . ."

Sitting alone in darkness, in the cold, in winter, she looked through a door into another world and saw there sun and freedom and air to breathe. And love, or something enough like love. And knew that she didn't have to stay in the cold—all she had to do was to stand up and walk through the door.

". . . then maybe after that . . ."

"No, Byron, I can't," she told him, not even wondering why she said it.

"Oh? Well, maybe I could stay over tomorow, and . . ."

"No. Not tomorrow either.

"Well, just tell me when you could . . ."

"Byron, I can't go out with you again. That's all."

"I don't understand you," he said. "What's the matter, Ellie? Everything was so great."

Only walk through the door. She shut her eyes. "I'm sorry," she said. "Please, Byron, I'm sorry. It's nothing to do with you. Just me."

There was a pause. Then his voice regained its easy assurance. "I'll call again, Ellie," he said. "This is probably a bad time for you to get away. In a week or two when . . ."

She pulled together all the strength she had left. "Don't call, Byron," she said. "If you do I'll just hang up. Goodbye."

She put back the receiver before he could say anything more and sat straight and quiet, holding the phone in her lap, for a long time, without thinking anything.

There was a lot to do at the library these days. When his new glasses arrived, Whit plunged into a fury of work. There were job reorganizations, book ordering, a neglected film collection to bring up to date, a budget argument with the library board. Ellie was glad for the work.

Then one day late in February a letter came for John with the address of the state prison on the envelope. Ellie handed it to him without comment when he came home from work.

He frowned and ripped the envelope open, pulled out a sheet of paper closely written, front and back. He sat at the kitchen table to read.

"Aaron?" Ellie asked. She tried to say the name as she would say any other. John nodded.

As he read his frown deepened. He finished, turned the paper over, and read it through again. Then he pushed it across to Ellie. "There," he told her shortly.

She picked it up. "Dear Mr. Clark," she read. The penciled writing was thin and wavery, but the letters were carefully formed.

> Please give this to Mr. Meade, too. I am sorry, but I am in the prison again. I don't like to write to you because I didn't think I would have to bother you any more. What happened was after I had been here a while I got real sick and they brought me to the prison hospital. The doctor told me I had to let them do an operation and take out my appendix. I asked if I would die if they didn't do the operation and he said yes. So I thought I've never been anything but trouble all my life for everybody I've known and so I told him I wouldn't have the operation. I just wanted to die. A lot of doctors and people came in and they were right mad at me and they all said I would die, so I wouldn't let them take my appendix out.

Ellie looked over at John. He sat quietly at the table, staring at his interlocked fingers. She turned back to the letter.

> It hurt so much I never hurt so bad in my life. I thought I would have to die from it. It went on for days and days. I don't know how long. They kept wanting to do the operation and I said no. Then after a long time it stopped hurting so bad and I didn't die.
>
> I'll get out of the prison March 6th. I can't go on any

more the way I have been. I don't want to ask you for anything again, or Mr. Meade. But if you will just let me stay at one of your places until I can get in that center then I won't have to ask you for anything else. I know I can do it this time. There isn't anything else I can do. I can't live the way I am. I'll have to kill myself some other way. I can't stand this. I won't come in your house if you don't want. I will sleep in your car.

> Yours sincerely,
> Aaron Avery Sloane

Ellie laid the letter on the table. She didn't want to say anything. She didn't want anything to show in her face.

John picked it up and folded it back into the envelope. "I guess I'll take it over to Whit," he said. "I'm not quite sure what to make of it."

He stuffed the envelope into the pocket of the coat he had never taken off, and he went out.

An hour later Ellie was wiping applesauce from Betsy's face when she heard the front door open, heard the earnest low voices in the living room.

Then Whit came into the kitchen. "Ellie, John's phoning the prison," he said. "We thought before we do anything we'd better find out if Aaron's telling us the truth."

Ellie helped Betsy to the floor and gave her a quick pat. "Run along now, baby," she told her. She sat down. "What a mess, Whit," she said.

"Well, we all knew we'd hear from him sooner or later." Whit fiddled restlessly with the bowl of his pipe. "I'm not sure this letter ought to make us change our minds and take him back. It is pathetic, though . . ." His voice trailed off.

Keith crawled out from his lair beneath the table. "Take who back?" he demanded. "You talking about Aaron? Mama, is Aaron coming back?"

191

Betsy, hovering still at the door, clapped her hands. "Aaron!" she squealed. "Aaron come back!" She galloped down the hall with Keith behind her, both of them giggling raucously.

Ellie watched them. Their world was so different. The Aaron they knew was only a kind man who had carved them boats. And he really was that kind man, of course, for them. All he ever needed from them was love. Aaron knows how to get love.

She folded her arms on the table and rested her head on them. Suddenly she was tired. The aloneness inside her grew until she felt it would stifle her. So many separate worlds. Keith and Betsy's world, Aaron's, John's. Her own. Worlds revolving past each other forever, never touching.

She felt Whit's hand cover hers. He cleared his throat hesitantly. "Ellie, it's none of my business," he said, "but I get the idea there's more the matter over here than Aaron Sloane. You and John have both been going around for weeks and weeks looking like ghosts. If there's anything I can do, or if you just want somebody to talk to, well, I'm here."

She turned her hand around to hold onto his. She was crying. She didn't want to do that. It took so little to start the crying, and she was so tired. Tired of crying, tired of every·thing. "It's nothing I could ever talk about, Whit," she said. "But just . . . oh, there's no way to fix it. Thank you for wanting to help. God, I wish you could." Can one world ever really touch another?

She got up and went to rinse her face at the sink, to smooth back her hair, to light a cigarette.

John came in. "I just talked to the prison warden," he said. "Aaron was telling the truth. It all happened."

"Everything?" Whit asked.

"Everything. Aaron was working on the roads when he doubled over and they had to take him to the hospital. Most

192

of the hospital staff must have been in there trying to talk him into the operation, but he wouldn't have it. The doctors really didn't expect him to pull through. The warden said he must be made out of cast iron. He's out of the hospital now, back in prison, but they're not having him do any hard work."

"So he was trying to die," said Ellie, low.

"Well, maybe. I don't know if I quite buy the suicide part. Somehow I have to think that if Aaron had been serious about killing himself he wouldn't have tried to do it that way. I think he would have found some way to do it that he couldn't back out of at the last minute. Or be rescued from. Something like a gun to the head, or a fast leap out a window."

He leaned against the door and rubbed his eyes. Maybe he even believed he was trying to die," he said. "And of course it just might have worked. I've heard of people living through appendicitis, but I don't think it's anything you can count on."

"Mightn't he kill himself now?" Whit asked. "Or when he gets out of prison? Mightn't he be that desperate now that he's lived through this?"

"I just don't know," John said. "We all thought Aaron was on the level at first, that he really wanted to change. Now I'm not so sure he is that desperate. More and more I think it's just a line. Maybe Aaron believes it himself, maybe that's why it sounds so real."

"But he's so sick," Whit said. "That's real."

John frowned and nodded. "I know," he said. "I know. That's what makes it so tough. He is sick and he needs help. But I don't think he wants help from us. Just free room and board. If he can keep on getting that, he'll never have to get real help."

Whit's voice was small. "Well, if you're right, then he probably won't ever be any different," he said, "no matter what we do. And he probably won't kill himself either. He'll just go on and on."

"That makes me feel like screaming," Ellie said suddenly. Seeing, not the table, not the worried faces opposite her, but a mountain of little white pills clicking one by one back into a bottle.

John looked at her strangely. She couldn't read his eyes. She looked away. She took another cigarette from her pack and lit it.

"Well, I guess we'd better tell Aaron he'll have to take care of himself," Whit said.

"I think it's the only thing to do," John answered. He pushed his fingers through his hair. "Lord, how I wish it didn't have to be our decision."

Whit stared into the empty bowl of his pipe. "Could we get a letter off to him?" he asked. "We could tell him that if it's really help he wants he can go right to the lock-up when they let him out of prison. He can get himself there. But whatever he does or doesn't do, we won't take him back." His voice scraped like chalk. "I'd like to put it in writing that we won't take him back."

"John," Ellie asked carefully, "did the prison people tell you what he's in for this time?"

John kept his eyes away. "The warden told me Aaron fought a Salvation Army worker," he said. "Hurt him some, not too much. But enough to get him in prison—he had a broken bottle or something. He'd tried to get into the Salvation Army home downtown that evening after I'd let him off. He was drunk, of course. The worker wouldn't take him in. The Salvation Army has a directive out not to let him stay in any of their homes anywhere. He's made too much trouble for them over the years."

"So he hurt the man and wound up in prison?" asked Whit. John nodded.

"The Salvation Army wouldn't take him in," Ellie said thoughtfully. "And we aren't going to take him in, either."

John looked at her. "We have to put a stop to what Aaron's doing to himself," he said. "If we can. And to what he's doing to us. It'll be all right. It has to be."

"Can we get that letter in the mail right away?" Whit asked.

Ellie stubbed out her cigarette. "I'll give the children their bath," she said. She moved almost blindly out of the kitchen.

She stayed a long time with the children. After they were bathed she curled up on Betsy's bed, with Betsy tucked in on one side of her and Keith, blanket-wrapped, on the other side.

The children's world seemed so easy. Even if she couldn't really be a part of it. Even if she could only hold them close and look into their world from the prison of her own.

Did you know there's a lock-up for each of us, Aaron Sloane?

She read to the children, told them stories, listened to them. Listened to the things she hadn't really heard in weeks.

"There's this boy in school, and he said a flying saucer landed right in his back yard. And he lives down on that street, you know, where Bobby Gilbert lives, and for a dime he'll let me look at it. Do you think there really is a flying saucer, Mama?"

"Mama, I find a bird nest today and no bird in it, and Keith said if I put it in a tree a bird will put his babies in it."

"Mama, is Aaron really coming back? Me and Betsy both want him back. We miss him."

Maybe another world is easy only when you aren't part of it.

Ellie held them, one with each arm, making answers, feeling the firmness of their blanketed bodies. Then Keith began to wriggle in her grasp and Betsy yawned hugely. It was time to let them sleep.

She went to her bedroom, thinking about the children, about John. About Aaron. About the Salvation Army worker who hadn't cared enough about Aaron and so had been hurt.

She thought about herself. She stood in front of the mirror and saw a sad thin woman with a colorless face. Not really a woman, she thought suddenly. A child where a woman needs to be. It's true what John said. A child growing older, never growing up.

Do you think you're a woman who can love a husband, love children? You, in the mirror?

The lips twisted on the white face. "I don't like you at all, Ellie Clark," she whispered. "You are sad and helpless and sorry for yourself and I don't like you at all."

Ellie. The mirrored face scowled. The name is Eleanor, but nobody ever called you that, did they? You know why—it wouldn't have fit—Eleanor isn't a child's name. You had to have a child's name, to warn the world that you are a child, to tell it to take care of you. Everything you do says you have to be taken care of.

And if they don't take care enough—if they don't care about you so much that they can't care about anybody else—then you hate them. The way you hated John. And had to hurt him.

She couldn't look at the mirror any longer. It made her sick.

She turned out the light and undressed in the dark. She sat on the edge of the bed, cuddling a pillow on her lap as she might cuddle a child.

She had wanted to die. Can't you ever learn how to live, Eleanor Clark?

She punched the pillow into mountain peaks. Well, what is living for, then? Ask that. What's the point to anything?

What are all the points to things people talk about? Happiness. But where does that come from, and what do you do when you can't get it or find it or make it? Love. Only you don't know how to love anybody, Ellie Clark. Just how to clutch at them.

Children. Passing life on. That could be a point, maybe.

The thought spiralled down and splintered again in pointlessness. Why do you bring up children? So the children, caressed and nourished and taught, can grow up and ask in their turns what it all is for? And, not finding an answer, try to see one in their children? And those children in theirs?

Doesn't there ever come a time when someone just lives and the living itself has meaning?

The point could be in people, all of them, and their children later, trying to build life; the way a house is built, or a poem. Trying and failing and sometimes, a little, succeeding.

But for what, even if they should ever succeed at all? Again the thought spiralled and shattered.

Some people said the point was God. She didn't know. There were too many questions.

Maybe . . . She traced the hem of the pillowcase with a finger. Maybe there isn't any point to it at all.

She set the pillow gently back on the bed. She lay down and closed her eyes. You're not really asking what life means, Ellie. So many people have done that. They've found so many different answers.

All you are doing is begging for a reason to live, yourself. Because you are going to live, aren't you? You haven't got the courage for dying.

SEVENTEEN

SHE MUST HAVE SLEPT. JOHN'S WORDS—TO HER, TO HIMSELF—
jolted her awake.

"This thing with Aaron has me feeling torn in two," he
said. "Anything we do can be wrong. I wish to Christ I'd
never met the man."

John was sitting up in bed with his arms clamped around
his knees. His face was outlined in darkness.

"There's nothing else you can do now, is there?" she asked.
"Don't you have to let him go?"

"God, what a responsibility," he said. His voice sounded
raw.

She reached out a hand to touch him, then pulled it back.

"You've done all you can do for him," she said.

Her own voice sounded far away in her ears, mechanical.
The air in the room was close. Something made it hard to
breathe. Outside the window maple branches angled black
against a closed sky.

Then she was saying, fast, without knowing she would
say it, "John, I'm sorry about what I did that night." She
pushed the covers back and got out of bed. She walked to the

window and turned to face her husband, a black shape in the night. "It won't help. But I have to say I'm sorry."

Her words lay on the darkness between them, waiting.

"You're sorry," John said at last, flatly.

Cold slivered in around the window pane. She felt it test the back of her neck.

"I'm not . . . I mean, it wasn't because of any way I felt about the man," she said. "It didn't have anything to do with him really. It was just that . . ."

Helplessly, she stopped. Just that what? What had Byron been for her that night?

"He just happened to be there," she finished, and shivered. It sounded like such a cold thing, such a hateful thing.

How would it have been if she had wanted Byron for him-self—for all that must be himself? But I didn't want him that way, she thought. I didn't even want to know what he was. It was a hateful thing to do.

"I did it because I thought I hated you," she said. "Oh, John, it wasn't any good. Even while it was happening it wasn't. I hated myself then, and it was awful."

"You hated me that night," John said quietly. "You hated me. Ellie, I ought to have spanked you that night. You were being a baby, a spoiled little brat. Sulking because I wouldn't take you to that damn party, running off to it anyway, going out with . . . whatever his name was. While I was fighting through that last hellish night with Aaron."

"Aaron." Like a door flying open, Ellie's anger broke through fresh, shook in every muscle. "Aaron. John, you have no idea how sick, how mortally sick I was of hearing about poor Aaron. When he called you up that night, and you went off to Mound City like a—like a trained dog, and brought him in out of the snow, and you talked about dump-ing him, but not till you'd done one more thing for him—one more thing—John, I could see it always being just one more thing! Forever!"

"I suppose you thought I got some kind of kick out of taking care of the poor bastard."

"I don't know what you got out of it. I just hated you."

She turned away, breathing the dank coldness of the window glass.

John's voice was measured. "That night, Ellie child, Aaron Sloane needed a lot more than you needed. What I was doing for him might not have been the best thing to do, but he did need help. Maybe you'd like to be the only one who ever needs help."

She whirled back to him. "I don't want any damn help from you!" she shouted.

Bedsprings creaked restlessly in the next room. She lowered her voice. "Oh, I don't even know what I mean. But why do you forever have to help, John? Why did you have to try to change Aaron? Why couldn't you just let him be what he was? Do you think you can save the whole world?"

"I thought I had a chance to help one part of it," he said. "Aaron can't stand what he is."

"Yes, he can! He can!" Her voice was climbing higher again. "That's what you and Whit were saying this evening. And you were right! Aaron wants to be exactly what he is. He just wants you to take care of him—the rest of it is nothing but an act. But you can't let him be the way he is, can you? You'll only take care of him to make him be different. When you find out you can't change him, you put him out!"

"Putting him out now is the only way . . ."

"The only way to make him change," she interrupted. "Make him change—see?"

"It's not likely he'll ever be any different, no matter what we do," John said coldly. "You don't have to worry about him. But as long as he stays here we're just letting him . . ."

"You mean you're just failing," she snapped out. "Of course he won't change, not here or anywhere else, but if you can't be a big man and rescue him then you can't stand the sight of him. So you throw him out."

She took a step back toward the bed. "You just have to be the big man, don't you?"

John stood up, stood over her. "If you're so goddamn sorry for Aaron Sloane, you write to him," he said. "Tell him you'll come and get him when he's out of prison. Tell him he can live here forever and you'll buy him his booze. Tell him you'll sleep with him, too—you might as well."

She reached out and slapped him with her open hand, as hard as she could, on his face. The sound cracked the darkness. Her hand stung when she pulled it back.

He stood a moment and looked at her. His eyes showed faintly light in his half-seen face. Then he took her hard by the shoulders. She felt his thumbs bruise her skin. He walked her back until she was pressed against the window glass. His arm muscles trembled with their tightness as he held her.

"My God, I hate you, Ellie," he said. The words squeezed out in a hard whisper. "I'd like to . . . My God."

His fingers splayed out and his arms fell to his sides, still trembling stiff.

Ellie rubbed her shoulders, watching him. "You've always wanted to change me, too," she said.

John looked at her in silence.

Then he walked away. She heard his hand moving among the things on the bureau. A match rasped and flared. The flame of it threw his jaw and the straight line of his cheek into brightness. Then the flame died and the tip of a cigarette floated redly, a disembodied thing, in the dark corner where he stood.

"You think I wanted to change you," he said at last. "Well,

I did. You've come at me like a child ever since I've known you. God, I've wanted you to grow up."

"I wanted you to take care of me, if that's a crime," she said. "You're right—as if I were a child. That's not what it is to be married. I guess I know that now. I'm—I hope I'm past wanting that. But I didn't want you to change me. I wanted you to take me the way I was. The way I was never was all right with you."

"How could you have been all right the way you were?" he asked shortly. "Ellie, you don't make sense. What you were was a baby. I wanted a wife—a wife! Not a baby."

"You knew what I was when you married me," she said. "Did you want me so you'd have someone you could change?" She turned to the window again, waiting for his answer. She cooled her forehead on the glass.

"I could ask you that question," he said. "Did you marry me to let me change you?" His voice cut sharp behind her. "Or did you want to show me up, Ellie? Did you want to show me I couldn't change you, no matter how hard I tried? To laugh at me for not being man enough to make you grow up?"

"I don't know what you mean," she whispered.

The black branches shaped a cube, a diamond, something that might be a face. A vast, cold face.

"You're a great deal like Aaron," he said.

"No. No."

Don't say it. Don't say it and make it true.

"No," she whispered again.

"You always were like Aaron," John went on relentlessly. "Only Aaron worked harder at it. He knew the rules better, he'd had more experience. Taking and taking—living off people like a parasite—laughing at them inside himself when they tried to help him. You just hadn't quite figured out what you were doing, Ellie, that was the difference."

202

The leering branch-face stretched grotesquely.

"What did you marry me for, Ellie?"

He demanded truth, but there were so many kinds of truth.

"I don't know," she answered, and it was true. Then, defiantly, "I needed you."

"Don't you think I've ever needed you?" he asked quietly.

She turned her face to where he was, not lifting her head from the window pane. In the dark the bright circle of ash plunged downward and was extinguished.

"I wanted a wife," he said. "I wanted to make you be a wife. No, I couldn't take you the way you were."

She heard his bare feet slap across the floor, cross back. Cross again.

"Maybe you're right," he said at last. "Maybe I did want to be the one to change you. I'm not sure. Maybe that was why I had to help Aaron, because I'd tried so hard to help you, for so long, and you had never been any better. I felt as if my life was . . . it was as if I didn't have anything to give anybody at all. As if I wasn't alive. My work . . . it feeds us, but it's not work that matters very much to anybody. There hasn't been any way I've mattered much."

"Does your life have to depend on your changing somebody else's life?" she asked. And asked him, as she had asked herself, desperately, having to know, "Can't people matter, just living? Can't they even matter to other people, just living?"

"I don't know," he answered.

Beyond the glass a gust of wind frayed out gaunt twigs like fingers reaching.

When John spoke again his voice was hard, choked off, as if he were trying not to shout. "Ellie, I hate you for what you did with that guy," he said. "I don't know if I'll ever stop hating you for that. I didn't know what to do when you told me about him. When I went out that door I didn't know if

I'd ever come back. I wanted to beat you up, I wanted to . . . kill somebody. Christ, I wanted to kill somebody!"

He jerked the door open and the click of the latch was an explosion. Yellow light bent in from the hall, then shrank to darkness as the door shut after him.

Stillness rattled in the room.

Ellie stayed where she was, held against the window, waiting. And then not waiting.

Outside branches stirred and lifted, the misshapen face tore apart.

There was no sound beyond the door.

Then, slow footsteps. Light streaked the floor and John was back. "Ellie," he said.

He stood just inside the doorway. "Even if you're right, even if I wanted you so I could change you, there was another way I wanted you, too."

"I've wanted you," she said. "I don't know what all else there's been mixed up in it."

"Ellie." He spoke sharply. "Come here."

She stayed by the window, not moving. "We've been hurting each other for so long," she said. "Have we got anything left?"

"No," he told her. "There's nothing left. Whatever we might have had, we've wrecked, I think."

He was beside her, touching her hand. "What if we tried to start over again?" His fingers dropped away. "If you want to start," he said.

"I want to," she answered.

Then unbelievably, they were together, and it was the way it had always been.

And it was a way it had never been before.

Afterward they lay, tired and complete, nestled to each other in the bed that had held them so many times. Her cheek nudged into his shoulder, his leg lay warm across her thigh.

"I don't want to say I love you," she told him softly. "I've said it too much, and I don't know what it's supposed to mean."

"I don't know either," he answered her sleepily. "We don't have to say it."

The twigs outside the window brushed a gently moving lacework on the quiet night.

EIGHTEEN

AARON SLOANE CAME BACK, OF COURSE.

He came to their house on the sixth of March, the same day he was released from the state prison. He waited only until evening, until he was drunk.

They'd all been half-expecting him. The whole day they had kept warning each other that he might be back. That he probably would be back. Keeping each other and themselves braced to refuse him.

Ellie had invited the Meades to dinner—it had seemed fitting, as if the sixth of March were an occasion.

But as the hours built up and dinner was over and the dishes were done and the children were in bed, they all began to hope a little that Aaron had given them up.

And then, of course, he did come back.

Standing just inside the front door, talking to John, Aaron didn't look like a man escaped from death. Paler, perhaps, than when they had seen him last, that New Year's Day. From somewhere he had picked up another old overcoat, an olive one.

Whit moved up beside John. His little eyes held steady

behind their glasses, but his forehead wrinkled sharply up to the scalp.

Grace watched from the easy chair, one bright fingernail scraping nervously at a ceramic flower pinned to her collar.

Ellie had come from the kitchen, had stopped halfway into the room.

Aaron didn't look at any of them. His eyes were gone out, dead, the way they had been before.

"I'm not asking much, Mr. Clark," he muttered. "Told you I'd sleep in your car. Just till they let me in that hospital place. Not the lock-up, the other one."

He ducked his head. "Won't take me in there right now—I been drinking some."

"We told you we wouldn't let you stay with us," John said firmly. "You can go to the regular mental hospital if you want to."

"Not your house, Mr. Clark. In your car. Won't make you any trouble."

John was standing too straight. His hands were jammed in his pockets. "No, Aaron," he said.

"Stay with you, Mr. Meade?"

"None of us can help you any more, Aaron," said Whit. He pulled the white-bowled pipe from his pocket and held it tightly in his hand.

Aaron's head twitched. "No more lock-ups," he said. "Can't stand lock-ups."

"I'm sorry," John said.

"Been all over town looking for someplace to stay. Isn't any place that'll take me. I hitched a ride out here. You've been real good to me before." Aaron scratched his head with fingers that trembled. "I won't bother you any."

He moved past the three of them and sat on the couch, heavily. "Can't stand any kind of lock-ups any more." He dropped his head into the palms of his hands. "Don't want to live any more. They'll have me in jail again by morning if you don't let me stay here."

"You'll be taken care of in the hospital," Whit said gently.

Aaron didn't seem to hear him. "Tried to kill myself before, but it didn't work," he muttered into his hands. "I'm still alive."

A muscle beside John's mouth quivered and tightened. "You'll have to go now, Aaron," he said. "I'll call a cab to get you to the bus station. And I will let you have bus fare to Cedarville. But that's all I can do for you."

He went to the telephone and picked up the receiver. He propped it with his shoulder and looked into the directory. The dial whirred.

Aaron raised his head. "I'm not going to that lock-up, Mr. Clark," he said.

He sat hunched forward on the couch with a hand on each knee. He looked as he had looked the first time Ellie had seen him. Tired. Hopeless. Defeat in the bones of him.

But patient.

"I'll kill myself," he said. "This time it'll work. Walk out in the street in front of a truck—knew a man once did that. It'll work."

"Yes, Walnut Drive," John said into the telephone. "Right away, please. Yes."

He put the receiver down and walked back across the room. He stood in front of Aaron, looking into the sunken face.

"You won't kill yourself, Aaron," he said softly. "Either you'll get yourself to the hospital or you'll get yourself arrested. One or the other."

Aaron's eyes, the hopelessness imbedded in them, met John's. "Don't you care what happens to me?" he asked.

John looked back at him, unmoving.

"No," he said.

For a moment life crept into Aaron's eyes. They thinned to slits, then dulled again and widened.

He turned to Whit. "Mr. Meade?" he asked, appealing.

Whit's forehead reddened. His chest pulled up as he breathed. "I'm with John on this, Aaron," he said.

Under the worn overcoat all Aaron's loosened knots of muscles seemed to gather together. He pulled up from the couch, suddenly tall over the other men. His eyes were slashes above his jutting cheek bones. His voice cut at them.

"I won't forget this," he promised.

His hands were fists at his sides, the skin of them drawn in between hard knuckles.

"I won't ever forget this," he repeated.

The words were spaced, each word a separate threat.

The slashes of eyes glared out at them all, holding them motionless, stopped. For a merciless time, stopped.

Then his eyes squeezed shut. His shoulders sagged. His whole body shuddered and seemed to shrivel to an empty skin. Tears crawled from the crumpled eyelids and furrowed down the sides of his nose. He didn't try to wipe them away.

"No," he said. "You've been good to me. I'm nothing but trouble. Never have been anything but trouble."

He dragged himself to the door. He tugged it open slowly, as if it were too heavy.

"You'll be rid of me," he muttered.

The knobby shoulders lifted and straightened, first one and then the other, as he went out.

They all faced toward the closed door, none of them yet able to move.

Then John turned and dropped down on the edge of the couch. He shut his eyes and pushed his hands up over them.

Grace shifted her weight in the easy chair. "Well!" she said.

Whit stuffed his pipe into his pocket. He took an ashtray from the coffee table, examined it, and set it down again.

Ellie came over to the couch and sat beside John.

"Are you going after him?" Whit asked.

John shook his head.

Outside, loud, insistent in the night, a horn honked. And, unanswered, honked again.

$4.95

Stranger in Our Darkness

Aaron Avery Sloane came at Christmas time. He was fresh from the state prison, a far-gone alcoholic, desperate, a derelict. No one knew precisely what his crime had been. But he needed help, and there were those who were ready to help him.

There was Whitfield Meade, plump now and rather effeminate, who was once nearly an alcoholic, though never so magnificently as Aaron. There was Whit's wife Grace, the motherly one, whose concern for Aaron seemed somewhat more than motherly. There was John Clark, whose life had never made a real difference to the life of anyone else. And there was Ellie, the neurotic child-grown-older, who did not want to help Aaron Sloane, who feared him beyond reason. Who, beneath her hesitant prettiness, beneath her fear, her conventionality, may have been more like Aaron Sloane than were any of the others.

Aaron Sloane asked for help, to change, to be changed. And there was change.